SPEAKING TRUTH TO POWER

Praise for the Book

'P. Chidambaram's compendium of his writings from the previous year is both candid and sagacious, rich in its detail and insight. Incisive, lucid and channelling his remarkable expertise in policy matters, economic affairs and Indian realpolitik, *Speaking Truth to Power* is an instructive read.'

Shashi Tharoor

Member of Parliament for Thiruvananthapuram, Lok Sabha

'From Thiruvalluvar to contemporary India's Gross Capital Formation, this is a book of remarkable breadth. Mr Chidambaram brings his keen intellect and professional experience in law and economic policymaking to bear on a range of topics of critical importance to India's economic development. For those interested in the challenges facing our nation today, whether or not they agree with all the arguments, this is a book that I will readily recommend.'

Kaushik Basu

Professor of Economics, Cornell University, former Chief Economist of the World Bank and Chief Economic Adviser, Government of India

'At this critical moment in our democratic life, logical, reasoned arguments based on India's foundational principles are needed as never before. Chidambaram deploys his intellect and experience to slice through the fog of power: his terse, factual prose at each step a reminder that there are other, fairer and more pluralist ways to think about our future. Every citizen concerned about our polity should read and reflect upon these commentaries on our current condition.'

Sunil Khilnani

Avantha Professor and Director, King's India Institute, King's College London

SPEAKING TRUTH TO POWER

~My Alternative View~

P.CHIDAMBARAM

RUPA

THE EXPRESS GROUP

EXPRESS BOOK SERIES™

Published by
Rupa Publications India Pvt. Ltd 2018
7/16, Ansari Road, Daryaganj
New Delhi 110002

Sales Centres:

Allahabad Bengaluru Chennai
Hyderabad Jaipur Kathmandu
Kolkata Mumbai

Reprinted from *The Indian* EXPRESS

ISBN: 978-81-291-5106-3

First impression 2018

10 9 8 7 6 5 4 3 2 1

Printed in India by Replika Press Pvt. Ltd.

CONTENTS

सत्यमेव जयते

FOREWORD

Discussion, debate and dialogue form the cornerstones of a vibrant parliamentary democracy such as ours. As the world's largest democracy, we must take pride in the fact that the Opposition has a vital role in making democracy work. As a strong voice of the Opposition, Mr P. Chidambaram is eminently suited to carry forward the discourse that holds the government of the day to account.

That he has a fund of knowledge is well known. I have always marvelled at his deep insights on various subjects, ranging from public policy to politics, economics to external trade and national security. His steadfast commitment to the basic tenets of parliamentary democracy and political pluralism has enabled him to earn the respect of colleagues and peers across the political spectrum. I have had many interactions with Chidambaram over the years, and in all these exchanges, his intellect, peppered with appropriate doses of wit, has shone through.

All these qualities are reflected in this publication which brings together his essays on a wide range of issues of public policy. The focus of these columns is on the state of the Indian economy. Whether demonetisation, the Budget or the Goods and Services Tax (GST), Chidambaram presents a scholarly analysis of each of the issues that have dominated economic discourse in the recent months.

I have always maintained that demonetisation, while aiming to immobilize black money and fight corruption, may lead to a temporary slowdown of the economy. Further, I have reiterated that we will have to be extra careful to alleviate the suffering of the poor—something that might become unavoidable while implementing reforms in the long term. In my opinion, the success of a disruptive change like GST will always depend on its effective implementation. In the months to come, based on the experience of actual implementation, the GST Council and the central and state governments must continuously review the design of the GST and make improvements. Only then can we hope to create one nation, one tax and one market in the truest sense.

While commenting on demonetisation and the GST, Chidambaram traces their origins, highlights their inherent flaws and offers suggestions to counter their deficiencies. He brings in his wide experience as the former Minister of Finance to be able to recognize when and how things can go wrong. With the help of statistics that tell the story better than words, he has shown how India's growth story was actually disrupted.

In a multiparty democratic system, every political party has a place and plays its role depending on the acceptability of its philosophy and ideology to the people of the country. At a time when politics has increasingly become acrimonious, with people ready to abandon argument for innuendo, Chidambaram's columns reinforce the importance of civility in public discourse and the fact that criticism must be directed towards policies and not personalities.

The articles on Jammu and Kashmir (J&K) and Gujarat are certain to force you to think, regardless of whether you agree or disagree with Chidambaram's views. His suggestions are worth a serious thought for an alternative approach to prevent further alienation of the people of the Kashmir Valley.

For readers interested in non-economic issues that go beyond the realm of Gross Domestic Product (GDP) numbers, interest rates, inflation and exports, I suggest that you read the very useful commentaries on children, hunger and the looming threat to privacy, among others. Chidambaram's policy suggestions are worth reflecting on.

Speaking Truth to Power is a collection of well-argued, thought-provoking articles on the gamut of issues facing the nation and provides a counter-narrative to India's political, economic and social discourse, with style and substance.

I am confident that the book will encourage much discussion and debate on the direction that the country must take in the years ahead.

PRANAB MUKHERJEE

INTRODUCTION

When I publish—courtesy Rupa Publications India Pvt Ltd—my third collection of columns in a row, my readers know what to expect from me. They wish to hear the reasoned voice of the Opposition in a parliamentary democracy. I am glad that I am considered one of the authentic voices of the Opposition, an honour that I shall always cherish. I think I have earned this honour for no reason other than the fact that I have written week after week, without interruption and wherever I am on this planet, for 156 weeks!

I am also glad to share with the readers that these columns are now available, simultaneously, in Marathi, Hindi, Malayalam, Punjabi, Urdu, Gujarati and Kannada, and I hope to add a few more languages in 2018. Needless to say, they are available on *The Indian Express* Online and on my Twitter account (which has many hundred thousand followers). Between the two, they have more readers than the number that reads the columns in print.

I have, therefore, reason to be satisfied, but I am not, and I shall tell you why. The purpose of my writing a column every week is not to see my words in print or seek transient fame. There are grave risks to political commentary: misinterpretation, criticism and abuse, the last mentioned response outranking the other two! Yet, if I have written every week, it is because I believe that, in a democracy, discourse is the only way for the Opposition to engage the government of the day. Unfortunately, engaging in a dialogue is the last thing on the mind of the government of Mr Narendra Modi. You now know the reason for my unhappiness.

Forty-three months in government have not made the BJP more respectful of parliamentary democracy or more accommodating of the views of other political parties or of sections of the people who have an alternative point of view. Every opposite point of view is dismissed. Every Opposition party is portrayed as a demon. Every protest movement is defamed. In my view, the BJP's confrontational attitude has greatly diminished democracy.

Not stopping at denigrating every opposition to the government, a planned and systematic effort is under way to capture as many institutions as possible, the most notable being the media. Never before has the media keeled over as we find it has done now. News stories have been withdrawn, editorials and editorial page articles have been pulled out, interviews have been junked, and editors have been summarily dismissed in order to please the government. Numerous journalists have told me that they live in constant fear of being fired and, given that alternative jobs are not available, they cannot afford to lose their jobs. The only option is to fall in line.

Institutions too have been captured. Every official in the government knows that the Central Bureau of Investigation (CBI), the Enforcement Directorate (ED), Income-tax, and now even the National Investigation Agency (NIA), have shed any pretence of being independent. Every businessperson knows that the midnight knock is a wink away; otherwise why would businesspersons observe the silence of the lambs when the prime minister tells them, to their face, that the public sector banks were looted brazenly in order to provide undeserved loans to them (that have now turned non-performing)? Why did no one stand up and say that loans that were performing as on 31 March 2014 have turned non-performing because economic growth has slowed down?

Let me say this, loud and clear: your liberty, your tolerance, your accommodative attitude, and your willingness to live and let live are under threat. The BJP's agenda—as well as the RSS's agenda—is not Development but Hindutva, and Hindutva goes beyond asserting the primacy of a religion. It is a project that includes establishing the primacy of one culture, one language, one behavioural code, one civil code, one thought and one point of view. The allurement for the citizens—especially the middle class—will be the beguiling assurance that the affairs of the State will be guided by spirituality. In every case except Maharashtra, after Mr Narendra Modi became prime minister, he has installed a *pracharak* (propagandist) as the chief minister of the state who was brought up in the RSS's school of thought. (Mr Fadnavis too belonged to the RSS and his father was a *pracharak.*) In due course, the line that separates state and religion will be rendered irrelevant. The government of Uttar Pradesh and, to a lesser degree, the governments of Madhya Pradesh and Rajasthan are unabashed in the use of state funds and state power to advance the Hindutva agenda.

Amidst all these exertions to promote Hindutva, the economy is the casualty. In seven quarters beginning 1 January 2016 and ending 30 September 2017 (for which figures are available) the numbers of Gross Value Added (GVA), GDP, Index of Industrial Production (IIP), Gross Fixed Capital Formation (GFCF) and credit growth are the following:

Quarter	**GVA %**	**GDP %**	**IIP Index**	**GFCF % of GDP**	**Credit Growth %**
2016					
Jan–Mar	8.7	9.1	121.4	30.8	9.3
Apr–Jun	7.6	7.9	118.2	31.0	9.4
Jul–Sept	6.8	7.5	117.1	29.4	12.1
Oct–Dec	6.7	7	119.3	29.5	7.0
2017					
Jan–Mar	5.6	6.1	125.1	28.5	5.4
Apr–Jun	5.6	5.7	120.4	29.8	8.0
Jul–Sept	6.1	6.3	120.0	28.9	6.5
Oct–Dec	–	–	–	–	–

At the beginning of 2017, the columns were based on the data for 2016. It was obvious to any student of economics that the growth rate of the economy had begun to slide. The government, however, was in denial. It is this denial that allowed a reckless adventure like demonetisation; no one had the conviction or the courage to stop it. As the year progressed, more data became available, including data for the first half of 2017. The Table above tells the story better than words can. A decline in the growth rate of GDP by at least 1.5 per cent, a stagnant IIP, a fall in investment as a proportion of GDP by 2 per cent and a credit growth rate that was the lowest in 20 years are the highlights of the Modi government's report card. It must be marked 'Fail'.

It was, therefore, natural that I wrote more often on the economy than on any other subject. You will find that 25 columns out of the 53 columns are devoted to the economy, demonetisation, the Budget and the GST. Demonetisation drew more people into the debate on economic policies than any other economy-related measure in recent memory. And when the GST, with all its flaws, was implemented without adequate preparation—and the criticism exploded—nearly every citizen had a view on the subject. While demonetisation and a flawed GST derailed the economy, they had an unintended benefit. The two issues brought home to the citizen the hard truth that, merely because the people had voted a political party to government, it would be too dangerous to let the ruling party and the government run away with the ball (of the economy) and kick it around as they pleased.

I think that realization led people to appreciate those who stood up to the government and spoke truth to power. That phrase, *Speaking Truth to Power*, more than anything else, accurately describes the columns in this collection. Hence the title of the book.

While the focus of the columns was indeed the economy, you will notice that one-half of the columns are devoted to non-economic issues. They are equally important, and in some ways will define India more than the country's GDP. If you wish to start with the non-economic sections, please read the columns on privacy, children and hunger. There are also the inevitable columns on politics. For most part of the year, the political developments were depressing, but the result of the election in Gujarat brought some cheer and the hope that there will be a change of course.

I believe I have been faithful to the truth as I saw it. I believe that the numbers that I have used are correct; happily, no one, so far, has questioned their correctness. I believe that I have not allowed the fact that I belong to another political party to cloud my judgement. I believe that my criticism of the government's actions was based on sound economic principles and logic. When I wrote on subjects other than the economy, I followed the same principles of fidelity to truth and unbiased criticism based on sound logic. I have also observed the cardinal rules of civilized discourse—politeness, moderate language and brevity.

I was overwhelmed when complete strangers would accost me and refer to a recent column. Thanks to the online version and the many languages in which they are available, the columns have acquired a large readership. I know that everyone in government who matters reads them although he/she will not admit the fact! The debate in the social media is sufficient proof that the purpose of writing the columns has been largely achieved.

If you read the column every week, I am happy. If you buy a copy of this book, I shall be doubly happy! If you begin to think seriously about the economic and other issues, that will be my ultimate reward. In the final analysis, the political system and the economic strength of the country will determine its place among the countries of the world. They will also determine whether being an Indian, and leading the life of an average Indian, in the twenty-first century will be a life of dignity, peace and prosperity.

A WISH AND A FAREWELL

WILL 2017 BE A HAPPY NEW YEAR?

1 January 2017

We should be happy that the Indian economy, according to the government, grew at an average of 7.4 per cent (new methodology) in 2014–15[1] and 2015–16[2]. According to the government's estimate, in the current year too, the GDP will grow at about 7.5 per cent.[3]

We should be happy that the Indian economy will be among the fastest growing large economies of the world. Currently, the Wholesale Price Index (WPI) inflation is about 3.15 per cent and Consumer Price Index (CPI) inflation is about 3.63 per cent. The fiscal deficit will be contained at 3.5 per cent as projected in the Budget for 2016–17. Foreign exchange reserves are at a healthy level of about $360 billion.

Causative Factors

As 2016 draws to a close, the whole country should be celebrating the state of the economy, but there is no joy anywhere. Why are the people sullen, dejected and apprehensive about the immediate future? The proximate cause is, undoubtedly, demonetisation (about which I have

[1]Revised to 7.5 per cent

[2]Revised to 8 per cent

[3]Revised to 7.1 per cent

written extensively), but there are deeper causes. The frowns on the faces of those in the government (and especially of those key officials who have chosen diplomatic silence!) tell a story that is very different from the boast of the 'fastest growing large economy'. Let's look at five of the causes:

1. The confidence of foreign investors has been rudely shaken. Foreign Portfolio Investment (FPI) is a standard metric. Until October 2016, net FPI was positive at ₹43,428 crore. In November and December, the flow reversed dramatically, and FPI outflow was ₹66,137 crore, leaving net FPI at negative ₹22,709 crore. The last time net FPI was negative was in 2008 when there was an unprecedented international financial crisis. If it was a 'flight to safety' in 2008, it was a 'flight from uncertainty' in 2016. Will the uncertainty end and the foreign investor return soon is the unresolved question before the government and the country.
2. In December 2015, the IIP stood at 184.2. In April 2016, it was 175.5 and, in October 2016, it was 178. IIP is an indicator of the health of the manufacturing sector. The decline in the index speaks for itself. The worst hit is the consumer non-durables segment which is down 25 per cent. The capital goods segment is down 6 per cent. We should not be surprised if the IIP for March 2017 is lower than the IIP for April 2016, making it a rare year when industrial production actually declined during the year. Whither Make in India?

Double Whammy

3. Credit growth is a measure of economic activity. At the end of November 2016, year on year credit growth was 6.63 per cent, a historical low, and we must go back many decades to find a lower level. Of this, non-food credit grew by 6.99 per cent. Medium-scale industries (textiles, sugar, cement, jute) are the segments where one could find regular, non-casual employment. Credit growth to medium-scale industries, year on year, has registered negative growth every month since June 2015. If we go down to

the small and micro industries, the situation is worse. Currently, credit growth to small and micro industries is at (-)4.29 per cent. Demonetisation was the last straw and many of them have shut down and thrown millions of workers out of employment.

4. While credit growth remains sluggish—indicating that there is little demand for investment credit—the gross non-performing assets (NPA) situation has worsened between September 2015 and September 2016 from 5.1 per cent to 9.1 per cent. It is, as the saying goes, a double whammy for the banking sector. Banks have few takers for credit and, at the same time, banks are unable to recover loans. The inescapable conclusion is that the promised revival of the industrial sector remains a promise and there are no signs of revival.
5. Exports are a reliable measure of the manufacturing capabilities as well as the competitiveness of an economy. Look at the value of non-petroleum merchandise exports during the period January to November in the past few years:

   2012: $218.79 billion
   2013: 228.26
   2014: 236.94
   2015: 216.11
   2016: 213.80

   While some portion of the decline can be attributed to global factors like Brexit and protectionism, the main reason is erosion of the strengths of the manufacturing sector in India. The stark truth is that when merchandise exports decline, markets are lost and jobs are axed. It is not easy to regain lost markets because some other country would have stepped in to meet the demand. Neither the prime minister nor the finance minister has rung the alarm bells about declining merchandise exports. We have not heard a serious conversation about ways and means to reverse the situation.

After Surgical Strikes

I have highlighted only five issues that are indicative of the health of the economy. It will be evident to unbiased observers that all five issues—FPI, IIP, credit growth, NPA and exports—have been adversely affected by demonetisation. So, if anything, the state of the Indian economy has become worse since the massive disruption caused by demonetisation on 8 November 2016.

I cannot end this column without making a brief reference to the price that we are paying for the other 'surgical strike'. Since the 'surgical strike' (30 September 2016) to end infiltrations and terrorist attacks, 33 security personnel have lost their lives in J&K. As on 25 December 2016, the death toll of security personnel was 87, which is double the number of 2015. RIP, brave soldier.

I wish you a Happy New Year. I sincerely wish that my wish will come true.

BID GOODBYE TO A BIZARRE YEAR

31 December 2017

I think every country must reserve a day for laughter. A day may not be sufficient for India, but we could make a beginning.

Laughter is provoked by a number of things. There are truly funny events and matters. There are inadvertent mistakes that cause mirth. I enjoy the cartoons and jokes that appear in print, some make me roar with laughter. *Dennis the Menace* is a particular favourite of mine. The social media is replete with comments and observations that make one admire the wit of the author. Memes are especially funny.

There are some statements and events that can only be described as bizarre. At first blush, one is furious. I react negatively too, but I have learnt to laugh at the foolishness and ignorance that are behind the bizarre. Laughter is the antidote to the poison that is spread by bizarre pronouncements.

The year 2017, to which we bid goodbye today, was replete with instances that were bizarre. Here are some examples that were so bizarre they made me despondent or ashamed or angry, but in the end I laughed them away:

Dangerous Pronouncements

The pride of place goes to pronouncements of those in authority:

1. Minister of State (MOS Home) found a doctor absent at a minor function held on Christmas Day. (The doctor was on leave for a few days.) The minister flew into a rage and said the doctors who were absent should join the Naxalites and 'we will then shoot you with bullets'. The minister may have been told that we had too many doctors per thousand population and it was a good idea to 'cull' the number.
2. A judge of the High Court of Rajasthan cited the Vedas as saying that those who kill cows should be massacred (I wonder which Veda) and went on to add his own prescription: declare the cow as India's national animal and punish cow slaughter with life imprisonment. If a judge says so, I suppose enough space can be found in our crowded jails.
3. A minister of Madhya Pradesh gifted 700 wooden bats (*mogri* is the Hindi word) to brides. The inscription read 'gift for beating drunkard husbands, police will not interfere'. The minister, in one stroke, struck a blow for women's empowerment, for prohibition, for the institution of marriage and for police neutrality in a domestic matter (even if some bones were broken).

Foolish Diktats

Diktats by whatever name—firman, fatwa, edict—are high on the hierarchy of the bizarre:

4. 'Women can't cut hair, groom eyebrows' read a fatwa of the Darul Uloom Deoband in Uttar Pradesh. Visit to a beauty parlour was forbidden. Beauty is in the eye of the beholder. Ladies, don't go to a beauty parlour, take your man to an ophthalmologist.
5. The village panchayat of Madora village, Mathura, imposed a ban on girls using mobile phones outside their homes under pain of a fine

of ₹2,100. Why ₹2,100? Why did the panchayat pick on the number 2,100? Is it because we live in the twenty-first century? Or is it the price of the cheapest handset?

6. 'Don't celebrate Christmas', warned a fringe Hindu group. The group should have revealed that they hate Christmas carols, will burn Christmas trees, and don't believe in Christianity's most important virtue—forgiveness. But let's forgive them.
7. The head of the Dawoodi Bohra community directed members of his community to 'use Indian-style toilets and host weddings at selected venues'. We saw pictures of persons breaking Western-style commodes. To sit or squat is the question. Squat is fine, as long as it is not open defecation.

Sinister Motives

Bizarre can be sinister too, but those examples don't tickle me:

8. Indira Gandhi Institute of Medical Sciences, Patna, required its employees to fill a marital declaration form. The employees were asked to declare their virginity and the number of wives they are married to. It was not clear whether the form applied to male employees only.
9. In Thiruvananthapuram, Kerala, a boy student of Class XII was suspended from class for giving a hug to a girl student who had won a prize. The boy remained suspended during the last four months. The boy has vowed to fight for his (hugging) rights. He has a natural ally in Prime Minister Narendra Modi. The prime minister should send him his best wishes.
10. A teacher couple working in a private school in district Pulwama, J&K was sacked on their wedding day. The school management claimed that their 'romance could adversely affect the students'. Did the management intend to say that the romance could 'infect' the students? The couple protested and claimed that theirs was an 'arranged' marriage (sans romance, to please the school management).
11. In the world of the bizarre, Mr Donald Trump is the undisputed

king. What better way to acknowledge the reigning monarch than celebrate his birthday. And that is precisely what an outfit called the Hindu Sena did on Mr Trump's seventy-first birthday. The event held at Jantar Mantar, New Delhi, began with a *raj tilak* ceremony followed by cutting a cake weighing 7 kg and 100 grams.

Have a hearty laugh, bid goodbye to a bizarre year and welcome 2018. May it be prosperous and peaceful!

DEMONETISATION

Although demonetisation was done on 8 November 2016, it cast its long shadow throughout 2017. I was one of the earliest critics of demonetisation. Through statements and interviews, I articulated the reasons why I thought demonetisation was a reckless act and why it would not achieve any of the objectives set forth in the prime minister's address to the nation. The government did not relent and the Opposition, including me, did not relent either. The three columns in this section are a reiteration of my views. You will notice that the questions raised have not been answered to this day!

WHITHER RBI'S AUTONOMY?

8 January 2017

The Reserve Bank of India (RBI) was born under unusual circumstances. A need was felt to 'regulate the issue of bank notes and the keeping of reserves with a view to securing monetary stability'. However, in 1929, the world had been hit by an unprecedented economic crisis—the Great Depression. The monetary systems of the world were in disarray. No one was sure what kind of monetary system would be suitable for India. Hence, it was decided to make a 'temporary provision' and that temporary provision was the Reserve Bank of India Act, 1934 (the 'Act')!

The RBI's main objectives in 1934 and now are the same:

- to issue bank notes; and
- to keep the reserves

An Immutable Law

Under the Act and through numerous amendments, vast powers were conferred on the RBI. The word 'autonomous' does not occur in the Act, but, over the years, the principle of Central Bank autonomy has been raised to the level of an immutable law. Under Section 7 of the Act, the central government may give such directions to the RBI as it may consider necessary in the public interest, but the power has never been exercised in the 83 years of the Act.

There have been times when the RBI and the central government did not see eye to eye. One governor resigned in protest. One governor was forced to step down. Overall, however, the RBI and the central government respected each other's jurisdiction and learnt to work with each other. In a closed economy and with little reserves, the RBI was known more as a banking regulator and tight-fisted controller of foreign exchange than as an issuer of bank notes.

Since 8 November 2016, of course, the role of the RBI as the issuer of bank notes has come into prominence. The RBI has the sole right to issue bank notes (Section 22). The RBI shall recommend the denominational values of the notes as well as the discontinuance of issue of notes (Section 24). Further, it is on the recommendation of the RBI that the central government may declare that any series of bank notes shall cease to be legal tender (Section 26).

In the current exercise of demonetisation, how did the RBI acquit itself?

Role Reversal

1. The government has claimed that demonetisation was announced on the recommendation of the RBI. One has to suspend disbelief to accept that statement. The prime minister's speech on 8 November 2016 made no reference to the RBI's recommendation. On the contrary, the government's and the BJP's spokespersons boasted that it was entirely Mr Narendra Modi's brainchild. It was an idea imposed from above and the RBI betrayed its mandate.
2. The decision-making process at the RBI was opaque and dubious. The RBI's Board of Directors should have 10 directors regarded as independent. Seven vacancies in that category have not been filled by the NDA government. The three independent directors attended the fateful meeting on 8 November. The recommendation was sent to Delhi where the Cabinet was waiting! How did the Cabinet know that the RBI Board would recommend demonetisation?

3. Dr Urjit Patel, the Governor, justified demonetisation as a policy action to 'turn around' the economy. None of the governors before him since 1978 had advocated demonetisation even when the economy faced grave challenges. Dr Patel embraced the idea, barely 65 days after he took office, when the economy was growing, reportedly, at about 7 per cent!
4. The RBI is believed to have told a parliamentary committee that the central government had recommended to the RBI (on 7 November 2016) that high denomination notes may be demonetised. Acting in haste, the RBI recommended to the government (on 8 November 2016) that high denomination notes may be demonetised! It was an unusual role reversal. The RBI has refused to release the agenda note for the meeting or the minutes. It has refused to answer the question if any director had demanded more information or dissented.

Credibility Dented

5. The RBI was totally unprepared to manage the fallout of demonetisation. It did not have sufficient quantities of lower denomination notes. It had printed only ₹2,000 notes that were not easily exchangeable. Besides, the new note did not fit into ATMs. The RBI started printing ₹500 and lower denomination notes only much later. A terrible idea caused more pain through terrible implementation.
6. The RBI has a Monetary Policy Committee (MPC) that was constituted recently after years of deliberation. Money supply is an integral aspect of monetary policy. The MPC was totally excluded from the decision-making process.
7. In his speech on 31 December 2016, Mr Modi ventured into territory where no prime minister or finance minister before him had gone. He directed banks to increase the credit limit for small industry from 20 per cent to 25 per cent of turnover and the working capital limit from 20 per cent to 30 per cent of turnover. He directed banks to provide 8 per cent interest on 10-year fixed deposits of senior citizens. The prime minister nudged the banks to reduce the lending rates. That

was on a Saturday. On Sunday, the State Bank of India (SBI) led the pack and announced a cut in interest rates! Every announcement by the prime minister scuttled the independence and credibility of the RBI.

The RBI has come under severe criticism both within India and abroad. I would like to believe that the RBI has not fallen victim to 'institutional capture' by the current regime. I would like to believe that years of nurturing the autonomy of the RBI have not gone to waste.

DEMONETISATION, A PROOF OF THE PUDDING

3 September 2017

It is said that everybody is entitled to their opinions, but not to their facts. And the facts are here, finally.

The RBI published its Annual Report on 30 August 2017, the last date allowed under the law. The report confirms what many of us had said—demonetisation was the worst example of incompetent policymaking. About ₹1,528,000 crore, by value, of demonetised notes (or 99 per cent of the total value of ₹1,544,000 crore) have been returned to the RBI. So, the main objective of forcing people with black money to suffer losses has failed miserably.

The Original Objectives

We were told that ₹400,000–500,000 crore of cash will not come back into the banking system. The RBI would extinguish those liabilities on its balance sheet and pass on the windfall as dividend to the government. And everybody, except those who had hoarded black money, will live happily ever after. That fairy tale is now over.

I had cautioned that none of the original three objectives set out in the government's letter of 7 November 2016 to the RBI and in the prime minister's speech the next day was likely to be achieved. *Fake currency* has surfaced, *terrorist activity* has not abated and *black money* continues to be generated and used. The objectives were unexceptionable, the chosen instrument was wrong and useless.

As the facts did not follow the original story, the story was changed repeatedly, and the propaganda engine was turned to full throttle. Bereft of even a shred of truth, the government's propaganda is now clearly in farcical territory. The situation is beyond Orwellian. Sample these gems from the latest press release:

Discovering Virtues

1. 'The Government had expected all the specified bank notes (SBNs) to come back to the banking system to become effectively usable currency.'
   - Were the old ₹500 and ₹1,000 notes not effectively usable currency?
2. '...the effective currency in circulation today is only 83% with full remonetisation having taken place.'
   - By printing less currency, an artificial shortage has been created. Many ATMs are not functional or dispense cash only for a few hours a day.
3. 'The fact that bulk of SBNs have come back to the banking system shows that the banking system and the RBI were able to effectively respond to the challenge of collecting such a large number of SBNs in a limited time.'
   - It is amusing that collecting cash is touted as an achievement. Next, counting the notes in nine months will be claimed as an achievement.
4. 'Since November 2016 and until the end of May 2017, a total of ₹17,526 crore has been found as undisclosed income and ₹1,003 crore has been seized. The investigation/scrutiny is going on.'
   - What was the undisclosed income and what will be the tax revenue can be determined only after assessment, adjudication and appeals. The government may lose many of these cases. The final number may be much smaller.

5. 'The government has already identified more than 37,000 shell companies which were engaged in hiding black money and hawala transactions.'
   - The government can only allege these things. It is for the tax tribunals and courts to determine whether the allegations are true.
6. 'The Income-Tax Directorates of Investigation have identified more than 400 benami transactions up to 23 May 2017, and the market value of properties under attachment is more than ₹600 crore.'
   - This is a pitifully small number, given the scale of disruption caused.
7. 'As a result of demonetisation of SBNs, terrorist and Naxalite financing stopped almost entirely.'
   - It would be nice to see some evidence of this. Data from J&K showed a rise in the numbers of incidents and casualties. The home minister said that 35 districts in seven states are affected by Naxalism.
8. 'Digital payments have increased by 56%, from 71.27 crore transactions in October 2016 to 111.45 crore transactions till the end of May 2017.'
   - There is an increase in the *number* of digital transactions but the total *value* of such transactions is at about the same level as it was in November 2016.
9. 'The impressive revenue collection under the GST is also partially attributable to the demonetisation drive.'
   - Pray tell us, how is indirect tax collection impacted by demonetisation?

Catastrophic Blow

10. 'Some people had expected a very large shock to economic growth on account of demonetisation. Their expectations have been belied.'
    - Is a deceleration of 3.1 per cent not a large enough shock? Under the United Progressive Alliance I (UPA I), the GDP growth curve was between 8 and 9 per cent. Under the UPA II and the first two years of the NDA, the curve lay between 7 and 8 per cent. Since demonetisation, quarterly growth (and hence annual growth) has

settled at between 6 and 7 per cent. The Central Statistics Office (CSO) numbers for Q1 of 2017–18 are worse: GDP 5.7 per cent, GVA 5.6 per cent and manufacturing GVA 1.2 per cent. Is that not a catastrophic blow to the economy?

There are some who believe that power creates its own justification. The rest of us are interested in objectively understanding the impact of a policy and will support it only if it benefits the economy and the people.

From demonetisation to polarization (in Uttar Pradesh) to chicanery (in Goa and Manipur) to child deaths (in Uttar Pradesh and Jharkhand) to mob violence (in Haryana), we are being asked to tolerate incompetence. The NDA is practising a rare and extreme form of politics that will ultimately wreck both social harmony and the economy.

DO GOOD; ELSE, DO NO HARM

12 November 2017

Rhetoric, bluff and bluster have their limits. At some point of time, the law of diminishing returns will apply, and the truth will be revealed.

A year after demonetisation, every justification trotted out for that decision has been rebutted and ridiculed. Let me begin with the justification that was disarmingly simple and had gained considerable traction: ending the counterfeiting of currency.

No More Fake Notes?

One year later we are told that out of the ₹1,528,000 crore (by value, of demonetised currency notes) that was returned to the RBI, there was only ₹41 crore, by value, of fake currency! That represented 0.0027 per cent of the value of the demonetised notes. Before you express shock at the paltry amount, read this too: 'The counterfeit versions have improved from easily identifiable in the beginning to highest quality in recent times', according to officials who track fake Indian currency notes (FICN).

Between August and October 2017, the Directorate of Revenue Intelligence (DRI) seized high-quality FICN of face value of ₹35 lakh in the two new denominations (₹2,000 and the new ₹500) in three separate cases in Mumbai, Pune and Bengaluru. On 8 November 2017, FICN of ₹4 lakh in ₹2,000 notes was seized in Mumbai. *The Indian Express* quoted a senior DRI official who said, 'Currency seized just after demonetisation was of low quality, visible to the naked eye, but the quality of the notes recently seized has improved and a common man now cannot immediately distinguish whether it is fake or genuine.'

To those familiar with the challenge of FICN, this is not a surprise at all. If one human being can harness technology to print currency notes, after some time, another human being can also harness technology to imitate the genuine currency notes. Hence, demonetisation was not the answer to FICN. If it were, every country would take that route but, in the last 50 years, no major economy has done so. That simple lesson was lost on the Indian government in November 2016.

Corruption, Black Money Thrive

The same could be said about the other two objectives declared by the prime minister on 8 November 2016: ending corruption and eliminating black money. Despite demonetisation, corruption thrives. Bribe givers and bribe takers are being caught regularly, often red-handed. Public servants are being arrested and prosecuted for corruption. There is no evidence that petty corruption, that is so widespread and is taken as the 'normal' in citizen-government interface, has been eliminated, or even inhibited, by demonetisation.

As far as black money is concerned, income that is taxable is generated every day, a portion of that income escapes tax and is used for various purposes—such as giving bribes, funding elections, paying capitation fees, betting, hiring casual labour, etc. Unaccounted money continues to be used in sectors such as wholesale trade, construction and jewellery. Needless to say, unaccounted money is the money that drives illegal activities like prostitution, drug trafficking, gold smuggling and arms manufacture.

Demonetisation was not the weapon to combat FICN or corruption or black money. Yet, the government wielded that weapon. It was a thoughtless and rash decision that turned out to be a colossal mistake and imposed a huge cost in terms of denting economic growth and heaping misery on millions of ordinary people.

The Ethical Issue

Adding insult to injury, the finance minister has claimed that demonetisation was 'ethical and moral'. I am ready to join the debate and ask a few questions:

1. **Was it ethical to heap misery on millions of people, especially 15 crore daily wage earners?** That number represents one-third of the working population and includes farm labour, craftsmen, street-vendors and casual workers. They lost wages (or income) for several weeks, were forced to borrow, and many of them are in deep debt.
2. **Was it ethical to destroy 1,540,000 regular jobs during January–April 2017?** The latest data released by the Centre for Monitoring Indian Economy (CMIE) says that another 420,000 jobs were lost during May–August 2017. Many of those who lost their jobs remain unemployed (unless the jobless have miraculously turned into job-creators as claimed by Mr Piyush Goyal).
3. **Was it ethical to force thousands of micro and small businesses to close down?** This is no longer a speculative theory. It is a fact. On the anniversary of demonetisation, true stories of closed businesses filled the pages of newspapers. Example: There were 1,500 units near the Tiruppur Old Bus Stand working as ancillary units for larger merchants and traders; fewer than 500 are still doing regular business, others are either shut or waiting for an order for several months. There are similar true stories from Agra, Jalandhar, Surat, Bhiwandi and many other vibrant industrial hub towns.
4. **Was it ethical to provide an easy way for converting black money into white as now discovered by the government?** The government has admitted that demonetisation and the note-exchange window actually facilitated conversion of black money into white money. The government has promised to track the offenders and punish them, something that is easier said than done. How many cases can the Income Tax Department investigate

and decide in a year? When will the Income Tax Appellate Tribunal dispose of the 94,000 cases that were pending before it at the end of August 2017? Hence the charge will stick: money launderers got an easy route to wash their black money and many of them may never be caught.

I recall *Kural* 551, which describes a king who does harm to his people. No elected government in a democracy has the right to inflict unbearable hardship and misery upon the people. In one of his works, Hippocrates said, 'Do no harm'.

ECONOMY

The main purpose of starting 'Across the Aisle' was to write about the economy. Many people are frightened by numbers; they should shed that fear. Numbers will tell the story about the economy in a way that words cannot. You will find in this section that I have used numbers extensively. Some numbers will appear repeatedly: GDP growth rate, GFCF as a percentage of GDP, credit growth rate, IIP and number of jobs. The arguments around those numbers will also occur repeatedly. In a sense, I have tracked the course of the economy from the summer of 2014 to the autumn of 2017. To readers who followed the economy closely, the numbers and arguments will be familiar. To those who did not, it will come as a shock how economic growth that was cruising along at 7.5 per cent was rudely disrupted and derailed. 2017 will go down in history as the Year that the Economy Tanked.

PREPARE FOR 'SLOW DOWN INDIA'

15 January 2017

There are four engines of growth: government expenditure, private consumption, private investment and exports. Two of the engines—private investment and exports—have languished for many months. Private consumption was strong and kept the economy humming. Since 8 November 2016, however, private consumption has taken a severe blow, thanks to demonetisation. The only engine that appeared to be running was government expenditure. In this scenario, what can be expected regarding the growth rate in 2016–17?

Loss of ₹150,000 Crore

The answer has been provided by the CSO of the government that released the advance estimate of GDP for 2016–17. The estimate is based on data till October 2016, that is, before demonetisation. The sobering conclusion is that economic growth will slow down from 7.56 per cent in 2015–16 to 7.09 in 2016–17. That is a hit of 0.5 per cent. The conclusion is in line with other estimates, notably that of the RBI, which pegged the decline at 0.5 per cent. There is sufficient evidence that, post-demonetisation, the economy will slow down further. I am afraid that my prediction that the GDP will take a hit of at least 1 per cent in 2016–17 will come true. That is a loss of ₹150,000 crore to the economy.

The CSO has covered its flanks by stating upfront that it has not taken into account the impact of demonetisation. The finance minister alone believes that the economy has not slowed down and that demonetisation will not affect growth in the current year (2016–17)!

In support of his claim, the finance minister cited the 'robust' growth in tax revenues up to December—43 per cent in excise, 23.6 per cent in service tax, 10.7 per cent in corporate tax and 21.7 per cent in income tax. It is obvious that the finance minister is preparing the ground for aggressive Revised Estimates (RE) for 2016–17 in the Budget that he will present shortly. It is also likely that he will present even more aggressive Budget Estimates (BE) for 2017–18. He is like the person who whistles when he has to walk alone in a dark alley! I shall reserve my comment on the numbers until after the Budget.

Stalling Engine

For the present, I would like to focus on one of the engines of growth and what the CSO's estimate tells us about that engine. It is the engine of investment. The critical number is GFCF, which is a measure of investments in the economy. The CSO estimates that GFCF will decline by 0.2 per cent in 2016–17. Actually, the decline will be steeper because, post-demonetisation, it is nobody's case that investment was stepped up in November–December or is likely to gain momentum in January–March. (Incidentally, for most of the years of the UPA government [2004–14], GFCF grew by double digits.)

A close look at the CSO's estimates reveals that for three consecutive quarters the GFCF has shrunk compared to the corresponding quarter of the previous year, and the rate of shrinkage has accelerated:

	2015	**2016**
	(in percentage)	
Jan–Mar	5.35	-1.90
Apr–June	7.11	-3.10
July–Sept	9.70	-5.59

We also have an estimate of investments by corporates. The data gives the change in net fixed assets. The picture is quite bleak. In the half-year ending September 2016, net fixed assets of corporates have shrunk across all major sectors (see Table below).

YoY growth/ Decline in Net Fixed Assets (in percentage)	All Firms	Manufacturing	Mines	Construction
Mar 2015	7.47	7.73	3.51	-0.09
Sept 2015	8.49	7.55	5.56	-1.36
Mar 2016	2.77	-0.98	-2.39	-5.78
Sept 2016	-9.36	-6.07	-12.68	-19.83

Other Dismal Indicators

Both the government sector and the private sector announce new projects and the projected investments in those projects are tallied every quarter. Between October–December 2015 quarter and October–December 2016 quarter, the value of government sector projects that were announced declined from ₹256,669 crore to ₹42,128 crore and the value of private sector projects declined from ₹119,475 crore to ₹86,645 crore.

All other companion data confirms the slowdown in investment: FPI turned negative at the end of December 2016 and credit growth plummeted to an all-time low. One thing is abundantly clear: investments are dwindling in value. Besides, the rate of decline is extremely worrying. In this terrible situation, demonetisation will make things worse. It is axiomatic that if there is a decline in investments, it will cause a decline in the growth rate of the economy.

What this means for the common people is fewer jobs, more layoffs or retrenchment, low growth in incomes, and fewer people lifted out of poverty. *Achhe din* (good days) are not around the corner, certainly not in 2017.

STATISTICS IS GROWTH: LET'S EAT STATISTICS

5 March 2017

The CSO is an honourable institution. Dr Pronab Sen, the former chief statistician, and Dr T.C.A. Anant, the current chief statistician, are honourable men. Ordinarily, one should have faith in them. I do.

However, what should one do when they appear to contradict each other? Dr Anant, after releasing the data for the third quarter of 2016–17 (October–December), has concluded that the GDP in Q3 grew by 7 per cent and the growth rate for the whole year would be 7.1 per cent. Dr Sen, after reviewing the data, has concluded that the data is deficient and the growth rate for the whole year is likely to be revised downward to 6.5 per cent.

Whether the growth rate for the whole year turns out, finally, to be 6.5 per cent or 7 per cent, it would be a matter of satisfaction—not self-congratulation or exuberance—for the country. That, however, is not the question troubling informed observers. The question is, 'did demonetisation adversely impact economic growth?' The CSO data did not answer that question.

Economy Slowing Down

The government had claimed at the beginning of 2016–17 that the growth rate would be 7.6 per cent. Suppose we assume that, after demonetisation, the growth rate will be 7 per cent. That is an adverse impact, and the cost of losing 0.6 per cent of GDP will be ₹90,000 crore. If the growth rate falls to 6.5 per cent, the cost will be ₹165,000 crore. Neither is a small sum of money. The argument that demonetisation did not—or will not—have a negative impact on the economy is hollow and puerile.

Between Dr Sen's and Dr Anant's, there is good reason to lean in favour of Dr Sen's conclusion. After the changeover to the new methodology, the CSO publishes estimates of GVA and GDP. GVA is an estimate; GDP is derived by adding tax revenues and subtracting subsidies. Let's look at the GVA growth rates during three years:

	2014–15	2015–16	2016–17
Q1	7.26	7.75	6.89*
Q2	7.91	8.44	6.69*
Q3	6.29	6.95	6.61
Q4	6.19	7.42	?
Whole year	6.94	7.83	6.67 (est)

**after downward revision*

Demonetisation affected every sector of the economy except three:

- It did not affect government expenditure and government actually increased its spending after 8 November 2016;
- it did not affect the monsoon that was bountiful and boosted agricultural production; and
- it did not affect the revenues of utilities because the demonetised notes were allowed to be used for paying utility bills and actually encouraged payment of old arrears.

Let's, therefore, look at the GVA growth rates after excluding government, agriculture and utilities:

	2015–16	2016–17
Q1	9.26	7.35
Q2	9.82	6.47
Q3	9.98	5.73
Q4	8.76	?

The conclusion from either table is simple and clear: economic growth in the non-government, non-agricultural economy slowed down since Q4 of 2015–16 and was on a decline in 2016–17. Demonetisation that happened in the middle of Q3 accelerated the decline.

Relevant Numbers

Adding tax revenues to GVA and subtracting subsidies to arrive at GDP does not reflect higher growth. If excise duties are raised in the course of a fiscal year, as was done by the government, it will bring in more revenues, but not higher growth. If subsidies are compressed, it does not mean higher growth.

Growth is best captured by numbers reflecting greater investment, higher production and more jobs. While the GVA/GDP data may have sprung a surprise, many other indicators point to an economy that is not investing more, not producing more and not creating more jobs. Compare the GVA growth numbers in Q3 of 2015–16 and Q3 of 2016–17. In the Mining, Manufacturing, Construction, Trade/Hotel/Transport/Communication and Financial Services sectors, the GVA growth number has declined sharply in 2016–17.

In Q3 of 2016–17, the IIP recorded a meagre growth of 0.2 per cent. Bank credit growth to industry was negative at (-)4.3 per cent. The ratio of Fixed Investment to GDP declined from 29.3 per cent to 26 per cent. By September 2016, net fixed assets of all firms had declined by (-) 9.36 per cent. The average plant load factor of all thermal power plants was 60 per cent. Yet, it is claimed that demonetisation has not affected economic growth!

Just as the GVA growth numbers for Q1 and Q2 of 2016–17 were revised downward, it is likely that the GVA growth number for Q3 of 2016–17 will also be revised downward. When data for the informal sector is also captured, the GVA growth number will be moderated and will be lower.

Unanswered Questions

If the government is confident that demonetisation has not affected economic growth, why is the government not publishing the data on the outcome of demonetisation? Why have the restrictions on withdrawing our money not been lifted yet? Why is the RBI still counting the old notes in the old-fashioned way? How much of the old notes has returned to the system?

Which objectives of demonetisation have been achieved? Black money continues to be generated. Bribes are being given and taken. Terrorist incidents have increased in J&K. Fake currency has made its appearance.

There are a number of questions about the GVA/GDP number. That number is not the answer to our questions about demonetisation.

HAVE WE GOT OUR PRIORITIES RIGHT?

9 April 2017

Governments will come and governments will go. The people are concerned not so much with governments as they are with governance. The hallmark of a government is its priorities.

The central government will complete three years in May 2017. In March 2017, a new government assumed office in India's largest state, Uttar Pradesh, that is home to one out of five Indians. The development of Uttar Pradesh, or the lack of it, has a huge impact on India's development indicators. I venture to say that the priorities of the central government and of the government of the largest state—especially when the same party is in power in both capitals—cannot be different.

No government starts on a clean slate. It inherits certain policies and programmes from the previous government(s) which the new government may continue or modify or abandon. Besides, there are structural issues that must be addressed by successive governments. The new government must also find the resources to implement its declared policies and programmes. I think it is fair to assume that every government tries to do its best. Whether a government has succeeded or not is a question that must be answered by the people.

As the NDA government is about to complete three years, we have important reports/official data. They are: Data of RBI; Data of Index of Industrial Production (IIP); Second Advance Estimates of National

Income and Expenditure; and Three Quarterly Employment Reports.

I shall share with you the main conclusions.

The Bitter Truth

1. The RBI data is for the period January 2015 to January 2017, that is, 24 months. During this period, gross bank credit to all industries increased by a meagre ₹7,413 crore or 0.29 per cent. This includes micro, small, medium and large industries. That is why manufacturing (in terms of capacity utilization or adding new capacity) and job growth are in the doldrums.
2. There is confirmation from the IIP data. Between January 2015 and January 2017, the IIP increased by a mere 1.1 per cent from 189.2 to 191.3.
3. There is further confirmation from the estimates of national income and expenditure. In 2015–16, growth in GFCF was 6.11 per cent. In 2016–17, the growth rate of GFCF declined sharply to 0.57 per cent.
4. And, finally, the employment data also brings dismal news. Three reports have been released so far by the Labour Bureau. The reports use the data gathered from eight non-farm sectors: manufacturing, construction, trade, transport, accommodation, IT/BPO, education and health. The first report was a baseline survey as on 1 April 2016. The eight sectors employed about two crore workers. The second and third reports covered the first two quarters of 2016–17 (April to September 2016). During Q1, the eight sectors added 77,000 jobs and in Q2 they added 32,000 jobs, making a total of only 109,000 jobs, notwithstanding Make in India and Skill India.

Irrelevant Issues

The state of the economy is a result of external factors, legacy issues, structural problems, policy decisions, regulatory efficiency, institutional strengths and weaknesses, and administrative capacity. The government of the day is primarily accountable, but the purpose of this column is not to lay blame but to ask a question: what are the priorities of the government of the day?

The answer stares at us. Open any newspaper or watch any TV news channel. The headlines that scream at our faces are about illegal slaughterhouses, *gau raksha* (cow protection) vigilantism, closure of liquor vends, anti-Romeo squads, racial attacks on black Africans, clashes on university campuses, Aadhaar made mandatory, triple talaq, building a Ram temple at Ayodhya, counterfeit ₹2,000 notes, etc. Rarely does one find a mention of investment, credit growth or jobs.

Three Priorities

The priorities of any government in the present situation should be:

1. greater investment, especially private investment;
2. robust growth of bank credit, especially to the credit-starved micro, small and medium businesses; and
3. generation of jobs, especially in the job-creating industries and services.

The three priorities are closely interrelated. Investment and credit—either both grow or both languish. Both depend largely on the 'animal spirits' of the entrepreneurs who are private citizens. Just as the foreign investor has many choices of investment destinations (India being just one), the big Indian investor has at least a dozen options. Micro, small and medium businesses may not have the option of investing abroad, but they have the option of not investing more money at all!

Large businesses can borrow from the bank or the market, but micro, small and medium businesses are entirely dependent on bank credit. Growth of bank credit is usually a good measure of growth of investment. The bitter truth is that during the two-year period (2015 and 2016), both investment and bank credit have been languishing.

The inevitable fallout is increased unemployment. That is proven by the data from the Labour Bureau. Creation of only 109,000 jobs in a six-month period in eight non-farm sectors (that provide the bulk of non-farm jobs) is an indication of the poor state of the economy. This must be viewed against the promise to create two crore jobs every year.

We need to get our priorities right. We need to hear less talk and see more action on investments, credit and jobs. We also need less noise on matters that are irrelevant to the health of the economy.

BEHIND THE CELEBRATIONS: NO JOBS, NO PEACE

28 May 2017

In a democracy, people vote a party (or parties) into government so that their 'lives will be better'. That phrase, of course, is more complex than it seems. What makes life in the case of one person 'better' may not be true in the case of another person.

Under normal circumstances, an election is fought and won/lost on *roti, kapda* and *makan* (food, clothing and shelter) issues. Other issues may intrude on the consciousness of the voter as she enters the polling station but, in normal circumstances, she will vote for more food, more job opportunities, more wages/income, better water and sanitation, better schools, better healthcare, better roads, better transport and so on. She will also vote for better security and a life without fear, without violence and without oppression.

In a multi-party democracy, a 31 per cent vote share undoubtedly qualifies as a clear mandate for the winner—the BJP led by Mr Narendra Modi—in the 2014 election. What resonated through the length and breadth of the country was *Sabka Saath, Sabka Vikas* (Collective Effort, Inclusive Growth) and the promise of *achhe din*.

Counting the Reforms

At the end of three years, it is natural to make an assessment of the government's performance. I have already written on internal security and Kashmir (7 May 2017) and on the rise of intolerance and the damage it is doing to the constitutional fabric of the country (14 May 2017). While those concerns are important, the more important concern is the state of the economy—and its impact on the promise of a 'better life'.

Achhe din is possible only through radical and structural economic reforms, the kind that were first done in 1991–92. Against that benchmark, I am able to identify three measures done or attempted by the Modi government that would qualify as economic reforms:

- The passing of the GST laws (with all their flaws).
- The passing of the Insolvency and Bankruptcy Code (IBC).
- The constitution of the MPC and the setting of an inflation target for the RBI.

All three are works in progress, but I place my hope in the success of these measures. Besides, the government has effected some incremental changes that any government would have done. These include liberalizing the foreign direct investment (FDI) limits in various sectors, allowing self-attestation of documents, and auctioning of natural resources consequent upon the judgements of the Supreme Court (although the economic costs of the State extracting a huge rent upfront have yet to be calculated).

More Hype, Less Action

At the end of three years, the economic report card of a party/government that has an absolute majority in the Lok Sabha has a rather modest score. Moreover, the reforms attempted so far have not powered the engines of economic growth. As I had pointed out in the column dated 21 May 2017, the government has not been able to revive investment (as a percentage of GDP) or boost bank credit or create jobs. Add to this agrarian distress, the structural problems in the delivery of education and healthcare, and the lamentable state of water supply, sanitation and electricity distribution—the picture is one of a largely unreformed economy.

Unfortunately, the energies of the government are dissipated in useless exercises. After making 'planning' a bad word, the government created a toothless NITI Aayog. The result: there is no body to rein in the soaring deficits of state governments and misallocations in state budgets; no body to draw up perspective plans for the medium term; and no one to present an alternative point of view at cabinet meetings. Another disastrous exercise was demonetisation. The post-demonetisation amnesty scheme netted a princely tax revenue of ₹2,300 crore, bribes are being paid and taken in the new currency notes, and fake ₹2,000 notes have already appeared. The only detail shrouded in secrecy is how much of the demonetised notes have come back to the RBI (which is still counting them)!

Other initiatives are mere slogans or acronyms. Clean India (Swachh Bharat), Make in India, Start up India, Digital India, etc., have made little difference to the economic system. Some ideas sit ill alongside the reality. A few Smart Cities (a stillborn idea after the Jawaharlal Nehru National Urban Renewal Mission or JNNURM was junked) cannot coexist with urban blight and urban decay in almost all cities and towns. A 100,000-crore rupees bullet train cannot coexist with ageing railway tracks and obsolete rolling stock.

Here is an Agenda

Mr Narendra Modi has a burning desire for greatness, but his government does not have big reform ideas. As a result, the government ends up doing big things in a bad way (e.g., GST) or bad things in a big way (e.g., demonetisation). Mr Modi should embrace new ideas irrespective of who proposed them. The Direct Taxes Code is a big reform idea. Likewise, the recommendations of the Financial Sector Legislative Reforms Commission contain bold ideas. Reconstructing the dilapidated delivery systems of education and healthcare will be a big reform. Deconstructing the bureaucracy is another bold and necessary reform. Throwing open higher education to world-class universities will be a revolutionary idea.

The central government still has two full years of its term. Mr Narendra Modi should stay at the wheel until the last day and not give room to hubris (like the Vajpayee government did). The third anniversary celebrations will indicate the direction in which Mr Modi and his government are likely to go.

CSO CALLS THE GOVERNMENT'S BLUFF

4 June 2017

There are three kinds of people who claim to have some knowledge of the state of the economy—economists, quacks and students of economics. I believe I am a student learning economics every day since Eco 101 in 1967–68. Most of my learning was on the job as commerce minister or finance minister.

My first teacher was Dr Simon Kuznets. I am proud to count among my teachers Dr Manmohan Singh, Dr C. Rangarajan, Mr Montek Singh Ahluwalia, Dr Venugopal Reddy, Dr Bimal Jalan, Dr Parthasarathy Shome, Dr Saumitra Chowdhury, Dr Jahangir Aziz, Dr Raghuram Rajan and many young economists. Those names should ring a bell. Each one of them occupied a key position in the UPA government and, at any time, four or five of them were available to advise the prime minister and the finance minister. Each one of them was a renowned economist and did not indulge in quackery.

Demonetisation was quackery. There was absolutely no reason to disrupt the economy by declaring, in a near-midnight strike, that high-value currency notes would no longer be legal tender. After talking to a number of people, I had predicted that the cost to the economy would be between 1 and 1.5 per cent. I am not happy that I have been proved right.

Opposition Spot On

The data released by the CSO on 31 May 2017 has proved that the Opposition was spot on:

- The Indian economy began slowing down in mid-2016 (beginning of Q2); demonetisation made it worse.
- GVA is the new metric. Growth of GVA declined from 7.9 per cent in 2015–16 to 6.6 per cent in 2016–17. The cost to the economy was 1.3 per cent. That is bang in the middle of the range that I had predicted.
- Between Q4 of 2015–16 and Q4 of 2016–17, the quarterly growth rate of GVA declined by an astonishing 3.1 per cent (from 8.7 per cent to 5.6 per cent). It was a man-made calamity.
- On the new base year of 2011–12, GDP declined by 0.9 per cent (from 8.0 per cent in 2015–16 to 7.1 per cent in 2016–17).

If you drill further into the data released by the CSO, you will find many other disquieting features. Core sector growth, which is a truer measure of industrial activity, fell from 10.7 per cent in Q4 of 2015–16 to 3.8 per cent in Q4 of 2016–17. Mining, manufacturing, electricity, construction, trade, hotels, transport, communication, finance, real estate and professional services declined. Of these, the construction sector, which is the second largest job-creating sector, *shrunk* by 3.7 per cent in 2016–17 (meaning, job losses).

GFCF as a proportion of GDP, at constant prices, was 29.5 in 2016–17 against 30.9 and 31.3 in the previous two years. The government had flatly denied a decline in investment and cited FDI numbers. That myth now stands exposed.

Three Major Failures

All these confirm the arguments I have been making for weeks—that the government has totally failed to address the issues of *declining investment* as a proportion of GDP; *sluggish* credit growth; and *non-creation* of new jobs.

These trends were visible in early- and mid-2016. Instead of addressing those issues, the government relied on the advice of quacks, kept out the Chief Economic Adviser (CEA), demonetised high-value currency notes, sucked out ₹1,544,000 crore from the system and sent the economy into a tailspin. The government tried to justify demonetisation by putting up three objectives—end to black money, end to fake currency and end to terrorism. The objectives were unexceptionable, the minor difficulty being that none of them could be achieved—or was achieved—through demonetisation!

Ending corruption was added as an objective, but in the light of numerous seizures of cash in new ₹2,000 notes from government officers, that objective was quickly abandoned.

Cash is Back

The narrative was then cleverly shifted to digitization and the impractical idea of a cashless economy. A lot of people were taken in by the surge in non-cash transactions. That surge was temporary because cash was not available. Once cash became available, the balloon of digitization was also punctured. Look at the RBI's data released at about the same time as the CSO's data. Electronic payments month-wise since November 2016 have been:

Month	Electronic Payments ₹(in crore)
Nov	9,400,400
Dec	10,405,500
Jan	9,701,100
Feb	9,259,400
Mar	14,958,900
Apr	10,960,200
May (up to 28th)	9,421,400

Cash is back, as the primary channel to exchange value. One day the RBI must disclose the volume/value of the demonetised currency notes that were returned to the RBI. It must also remonetise the economy sufficiently to meet the needs of the people. When both numbers will be known, the believers in demonetisation will realize that India is back to the pre-8 November 2016 days and will ask the inevitable question: 'What purpose did demonetisation serve except to disrupt the economy and heap misery upon millions of people?'

It is time for the government to stop fooling the people that all's well with the economy and that the current policies are working. They are not. The government must get on with the job of reviving the economy by relying on the advice of truly knowledgeable economists. They can start with the only one they have, Dr Arvind Subramanian.

THE MAKE IN INDIA FLOP SHOW

11 June 2017

No large country can become rich without manufacturing the goods that are consumed or demanded by its people. Most services—especially the basic, low-technology and low value-added services—will anyway be produced within the country. A country will move up the ladder of prosperity if it can manufacture the goods and produce the services required by its people and also export a considerable part of those goods and services.

Prime Minister Narendra Modi was therefore absolutely right when he stated that his government's goal was to give the highest priority to 'Make in India' and called upon the world's manufacturing companies to 'Come and make in India'.

Manufacturing Gains Ground

The share of manufacturing in India's GDP is about 16.5 per cent. Agriculture has declined steeply and the Services sector has risen sharply. Apart from the changes in the shares of the two sectors, manufacturing has gained ground. Seventy per cent of manufacturing units are in the private sector and about one-third of those are with the quasi-corporate and unorganized entities. Manufacturing's share of GDP has risen steadily from 9.8 per cent in the 1950s to about 16.2 per cent in the 2010s. Mr Modi promised a further boost to manufacturing.

To make a product and capture a significant market share is not an easy task. There may already be one or more persons making the same product. It may be imported too. To be successful, the intending manufacturer must make it better or cheaper or reach it to the consumer sooner or be able to offer something which makes his product more attractive to the consumer. It is here that we face the hurdle of 'factor costs'. Land, labour, electricity, technology, transport, cost of capital, cost of borrowing, and many others are factor costs. Unless some or all factor costs are favourable, no one will embark upon manufacturing.

The major manufacturing economies of the world have reached their positions by making factor costs more advantageous if the products were made in their countries rather than made elsewhere. Making in a country must provide a 'competitive advantage' to the manufacturer. Take cars. They were first mass-manufactured in the United States. When Germany and Japan emerged as major economies, they offered competitive advantages and the industry shifted to Germany and Japan. A few decades later, car manufacturing moved to South Korea. A couple of decades later, a significant portion of car manufacturing shifted to India.

The shift to India was not fortuitous. It was because of a well-thought-out strategy that was translated into clear policies. That story which began in 1991–92 deserves to be told separately.

When Mr Modi promised to make India into a global hub of manufacturing, I assumed that he had been advised—and he had reflected—on the many hurdles that had to be crossed. I refuse to believe that 'Make in India' was just another slogan to enthuse the large gathering on Independence Day, 2015.

The Steep Decline

Two years later, what is the status of 'Make in India'?

The CSO has released the quarterly growth rates of GVA of manufacturing at constant prices (2011–12). I have placed them alongside the growth of overall GVA:

	2015–16	2016–17	2015–16	2016–17
	(Manufacturing GVA)		(Overall GVA)	
Q1	8.2	10.7	7.6	7.6
Q2	9.3	7.7	8.2	6.8
Q3	13.2	8.2	7.3	6.7
Q4	12.7	5.3	8.7	5.6

Since the announcement of 'Make in India' on 15 August 2015, there is no evidence that manufacturing has gathered momentum. On the contrary, it seems to have lost steam, and in 2016–17 the sector weakened considerably. Between Q1 and Q4 of 2016–17, the growth rate of manufacturing GVA halved. The weakness of the manufacturing sector is reflected in the steady drop in the growth rate of overall GVA.

The conclusion is that apart from the announcement of 'Make in India', there has been little policy or administrative support. All other data point to the same conclusion. In the five quarters between Q4 of 2015–16 and Q4 of 2016–17, GFCF as a proportion of GDP declined—30.8, 31.0, 29.4, 29.4 and 28.5. A drop of 2.3 per cent in 12 months is a disaster. Considering that GFCF was 34–35 per cent only a few years ago and the government has done nothing to step up private as well as pubic investment, it is a catastrophe.

Data Point to Flop

Data on IIP point to the same conclusion. In May 2014, the index was 183.5, in August 2015 it was 184.8, in March 2016 it was 208.1 and in February 2017 it had fallen to 190.1.

Data on credit growth point to the same conclusion. Credit growth to the industry sector has been negative since October 2016. Credit growth to micro/small and medium industries has been negative since March 2016 and June 2015 respectively.

Data on job creation point to the same conclusion. The eight leading job-creating industries created only 109,000 jobs during the period

April–September 2016. That is a sign of stagnation.

Data on electricity demand point to the same conclusion. The average Plant Load Factor of thermal plants is about 60 per cent, reflecting poor demand for electricity.

I had welcomed 'Make in India'. It was innovative and aspirational. Unfortunately, it appears that there was little homework done before and practically no policy support after. 'Make in India' has turned out to be a hollow slogan.

FARM SECTOR ON THE BOIL

18 June 2017

Farmers' agitations are spreading across many states. It is the culmination of the acute distress in the farm sector that many observers have written and spoken about in the last two years.

Two years of drought in many states was the main cause. The governments cannot be blamed for the occurrence of drought, but governments are solely responsible for the mismanagement of the consequences of drought. Apart from the natural calamity of drought, there were man-made calamities, and this column is about how the two have brought about the explosive situation in the country.

The bulk of farmers in India have no choice but to do farming. Land is the only asset they have, farming is the only skill they possess, and unless they grow food many of them will face starvation. Agriculture, despite its declining share in total output (GDP), is also the largest employer. In India's economy, the agriculture sector has primacy.

The Price of Neglect

Unfortunately, the NDA government lost sight of this basic truth. The agriculture portfolio is the Cinderella of this government. The Minister of Agriculture, unchanged since May 2014, is a political lightweight with little clout within the government. (How many of you can name Mr Sharad

Pawar's successor?) The minister has been neither seen nor heard by most people. The only memorable statement on agriculture that I can recall was when he repeated the prime minister's promise to 'double farmers' income in 6 years', and when asked if they had meant 'real' income or 'nominal' income, there was deafening silence.

On the other hand, the government erred grievously on the issue of minimum support prices (MSPs). In its manifesto and in the election campaign, the BJP had unequivocally promised that it would implement the M.S. Swaminathan Committee's recommendation that MSP should be cost plus 50 per cent. In government, the BJP not only reneged on its promise, it dealt a body blow to farmers by denying them even a reasonable increase in MSP in its first three years. The numbers speak for themselves:

	2004–05	2013–14	2016–17
	(UPA 10 years)		(NDA 3 years)
	Rupees per unit		
Sugarcane	74.5	210/220	230
Maize	525	1,310	1,365
Soyabean	1,000	2,560	2,675
Groundnut	1,500	4,000	4,120
Wheat	630	1,350	1,625
Paddy	560	1,310	1,470

The ostensible reason for denying a fair MSP was that higher MSP fuelled inflation, which is partly true, but to lean in favour of inflation control against the interest of India's farmer-producers was the height of folly. Some inflation is inevitable, and the government and the RBI must use other instruments to moderate inflation rather than reduce the farming community to penury.

Errors Galore

The second grave error was demonetisation. Mr Harish Damodaran has convincingly demonstrated how demonetisation has crippled the post-harvest agricultural economy (see 'The Crops of Wrath', *The Indian Express,* 12 June 2017). Agricultural products are bought and sold largely in cash. Demonetisation dried up liquidity and prices have crashed. According to Mr Damodaran, never before have prices of tomato, potato and onion crashed at the same time. Same is the situation with soyabean, arhar (split red gram), garlic, methi (fenugreek) and grapes. Noting that farmers have resorted to 'fire sales', Mr Damodaran's conclusion is, 'We have entered deflation territory in farm produce, whose proximate trigger clearly has been demonetisation.'

The third error was when the prime minister announced, on behalf of the yet-to-be-elected Uttar Pradesh government, that all farm loans in the state will be waived if the BJP formed the government. More likely, it was just an election promise in a state that the BJP perhaps did not expect to win, but it was an unequivocal promise that has returned to haunt the BJP in several states. Farm loan waivers are neither intrinsically 'good' nor 'bad'. As Dr M.S. Swaminathan said on 13 June 2017, 'Loan waivers, *though temporarily necessary*, do not provide for a secure long-term credit system' (emphasis supplied). When farmers do not get a fair and reasonable price and are unable to repay their loans, they demand a loan waiver. If the holder of the highest political office had promised a total loan waiver, why blame the farmers for demanding that the promise be implemented?

In February 2008, the fiscal situation was excellent, growth had found a new momentum, and a one-time loan forgiveness to small and medium farmers was justified. The central government was confident it could fund the waiver and so it went ahead and announced it. In 2017, however, every prudent norm was turned on its head. The prime minister promised a loan waiver on behalf of a yet-to-be-elected state government, no one seems to have examined the capacity of Uttar Pradesh to bear the burden, and no one seems to have factored the fallout in other states. Having mounted a tiger, the BJP does not know how to dismount it. Meanwhile, the tiger is galloping through Madhya Pradesh, Chhattisgarh, Punjab, Haryana, Maharashtra and Gujarat.

Jobless Youth Angry

The last straw was jobless growth. Young men can find no work on farms or off farms. Micro, small and medium businesses are not offering new jobs. Tier 2, 3 and 4 towns are full of jobless youth and their anger has turned against the central government.

The BJP will not admit its mistakes. Nor will any BJP leader tell the prime minister that mistakes were made. Will the prime minister pull a rabbit out of the hat? Wait and see.

INDIA AT 70: THE ECONOMY

13 August 2017

Freedom, a written Constitution, parliamentary system of government, and rule of law have several purposes and objectives: one of the foremost is that they will lead to the social and economic progress of the people of a country.

Imagine taking responsibility for the governance of a country in 1947 when 83 per cent of the population was illiterate, life expectancy at birth was 32 years, per capita income at current prices was ₹247, and per capita consumption of electricity was 16.3 kWh per year. Lesser mortals would have concluded that India was ungovernable. Any other Father of the Nation would have seized absolute power and done his best—or worst—to run a government according to his whims.

Not Mahatma Gandhi, who did not aspire to be in the government and preferred to serve the people in his own way. Not Jawaharlal Nehru, Vallabhbhai Patel and others who bravely shouldered the awesome responsibility of governing a vast and volatile nation.

Markers of Success

India has come a long way since 15 August 1947. Only the blind—and the bhakts (no intent to disrespect)—will argue that nothing, *absolutely nothing*, was accomplished in the last 70 years. They refuse to acknowledge—

- the rise in life expectancy at birth to 68.34 years;
- the rise of per capita income (at current prices) to ₹103,219 per year;
- the rise in literacy to 73 per cent;
- the reduction in the proportion of people living in poverty to less than 22 per cent;
- the self-sufficiency in foodgrains and the avoidance of famine;
- the conquest of plague, kala-azar, smallpox and polio;
- the advances in science and technology, especially space and atomic energy, with limited resources.

Every major political party of India had a role to play in the development story. The Congress was at the head of the central government for nearly 55 years. Non-Congress parties ruled for 15 years; of these, the BJP was/is at the head of the central government for nine years (Mr Vajpayee and Mr Modi).

Governance of India is not by the central government alone. State governments have an equal responsibility. Matters directly affecting the lives of the people fall under the authority of the state governments (see Constitution, Seventh Schedule, List II). Because governance at the state level is so uneven, development at the state level is also terribly uneven. As on 31 March 2017, the per capita income of Delhi was ₹249,004 and of Goa was ₹242,745, while the per capita income of Bihar was ₹31,380 (base year: 2014–15).

Who has been in the government in the poorest states of India? The Congress has not been in power in Uttar Pradesh since 1989; in Odisha since 2000; in West Bengal since 1977; and in Bihar since 1990 (it was a minor partner for 20 months until July 2017). The Congress can, therefore, be hardly blamed for their poor governance in recent decades. On the other hand, the BJP was in power in Uttar Pradesh during 1997–2002 and again since this year; the BJP shared power in Odisha during 2000–09; and the BJP shared power in Bihar during 2005–14 and shares power again now.

Five Indicators

It is time to do a health check of the economy as free India completes 70 years:

- **Jobs:** There is more evidence that we have jobless growth. According to the CMIE, between January and April 2017, the economy shed 1.5 million formal sector jobs.
- **GDP Growth:** There is a steady decline in the growth rate of GVA since Q4 of 2015–16 and, correspondingly, in the growth rate of GDP.
- **Investment:** In the 12-month period from Q4 of 2015–16 to Q4 of 2016–17, GFCF at constant prices fell from 30.8 per cent to 28.5 per cent. It was 32.6 per cent in 2013–14 and had touched a high of 34.31 per cent in 2011–12 (base year: 2011–12).
- **Credit Growth:** 2016–17 ended with a credit growth rate of 8.16 per cent, which was less than one-half of the average annual growth rate during the last 10 years.
- **Industrial Production:** In the last three years, the IIP has moved, sluggishly, from 111 in May 2014 to 119.6 in June 2017.

Celebration Without Joy

These are the five indicators that should be on the dashboard of the prime minister and the finance minister but, apparently, they are not. Both talk on everything under the sky except on the economy. The prime minister has the talent to turn attention away from a catastrophic economic situation to political issues. The finance minister is happy to throw out some inconsequential statistics that carry no credibility with economists of repute. There is no more than one person in the government who will speak truth to power at least occasionally.

Yet the government will lead the 'celebration' of India at 70. Who will join them? Not the 22 per cent at the bottom of the pyramid, not the farmers, not the manufacturers of goods or their workers, not the lenders or the potential borrowers, not the young jobseekers, not those denied education loans and higher education, not women, not the Dalits, and not the minorities. It will be a celebration without joy.

INDIA AT 70: THE ECONOMY (CONTINUED)

20 August 2017

I am happy to read well-reasoned articles on India at 70 and particularly about the state of the economy. In my interactions with people, village folk and town folk, I find that there is growing interest in matters like prices, jobs and infrastructure. At political rallies, I find that people don't pay much attention to political stump speeches or party-bashing or name-calling. They listen keenly to speeches about unfulfilled election promises; prices of farm produce, fuel and transport; jobs; the infrastructure deficit; education loans; and so on. Hence, I decided to stay this week with the subject of 'Economy'.

There is ample *officially blessed* material on the state of the economy. We have the Economic Survey, Volume 2 (ES) and the RBI's Monetary Policy Statement of 2 August 2017.

My dashboard in the column of 13 August 2017, had five metrics or measures on the health of the economy.

Jobless and Slow Growth

The first metric was **Jobs**. The ES has no separate section on jobs, only a two-page write-up on 'Employment and Skill Development'. The ES has given no numbers on the jobs created, except a claim that among those who received skill training, 427,470 persons were given employment!

Nothing is mentioned about the states or sectors which have created the 427,470 jobs. Nothing has been said about the number of jobs likely to be created in 2017–19. The silence on the most challenging issue tells the truth: India is witnessing moderate, but jobless, growth.

The second metric was **GDP Growth**. The ES admits that GDP growth declined from 8 per cent in 2015–16 to 7.1 per cent in 2016–17. It also admits that growth in the first half of 2016–17 was 7.7 per cent and 6.5 per cent in the second half. The decline, therefore, is from a rate of growth of 8 per cent to 6.5 per cent—exactly what I had predicted would be the impact of demonetisation. The GVA numbers are worse: in Q4 of 2016–17 it was 5.6 per cent. Going forward, the ES warns 'sustaining current growth trajectory (*read 6.5 per cent*) will require action on more normal drivers of growth such as (private) investment and exports and cleaning up of balance sheets to facilitate credit growth'.

Declining Graphs

The third measure was **Investment**. In two startling graphs (Figures 47 and 48), the ES presents a depressing picture of GFCF. Growth in Public GFCF has been on the decline since Q2 of 2015–16. Growth in Private GFCF has also been on the decline since the same time and entered negative territory in Q4 of 2015–16 where it remained through 2016–17. The forecast is even more depressing: 'The investment spending of the general government, relative to GDP, is likely to decline in 2017–18 as per available Budget information.'

The fourth metric was **Credit Growth**. I need say no more than quote from the ES: 'The high growth observed in the 2003–08 period was accompanied by a surge in credit growth, which usually exceeded the 20 per cent mark year on year. After being impacted sharply by the global financial crisis and the fiscal stimuli over the period 2008–10, credit growth remained around the 15 per cent mark till February 2014. Subsequently, it has slowed down. During 2016–17, gross bank credit outstanding grew at around 7 per cent on an average. The latest reading for May 2017 is 4.1 per cent.' Non-food credit growth as a whole as well as credit growth to agriculture, industry, services and personal loans have been on the decline since September 2016. The worst affected is 'industry' where credit growth has been negative since September 2016. Public sector banks' credit to industry has been negative since March 2016; it is only private banks that are giving some credit to industry.

The fifth measure was **Industrial Production**. According to the ES, 'industrial performance has declined from 8.8 per cent during 2015–16 to 5.6 per cent in 2016–17.' The IIP numbers are confusing. Going by the old series (base year 2004–05), the growth rate of IIP has improved from 0.7 per cent in Q1 to 1.9 per cent in Q4 of 2016–17. However, under the new series (base year 2011–12), the growth rate has declined in 2016–17 from 7.8 per cent in Q1 to 2.9 per cent in Q4! The new series numbers, although on a declining curve, are still better than the old series numbers! The new series numbers present a flattering picture which one may believe at one's own risk!

Given up on 2019

The RBI's monetary policy statement has confirmed many of the conclusions. According to the RBI, business sentiment reflects expectations of moderation of activity in Q2 of 2017–18 (*read slower growth*). Industrial performance has weakened and there is output contraction in consumer durables and capital goods (*read declining industrial production*). The number of new investment announcements fell to a 12-year low in Q1 of 2016–17 and high levels of stress in twin balance sheets—banks' and corporations'—are likely to deter new investment, and states may cut back on capital expenditure (*read sluggish investment*). The statement was silent on jobs and credit growth.

As I had feared, we are celebrating the seventieth anniversary of Independence without joy. I am afraid the government fears looking at the dashboard. It seems to have given up on *achhe din* by 2019 and is busy polishing the rhetoric of a New India in 2022!

CLUELESS IN NEW DELHI

17 September 2017

The time for boasts is over. India is no longer the fastest growing large economy of the world. Our misguided jibe against China lasted all of seven quarters.

In five successive quarters, the growth rates of GDP and GVA have declined (see graph below):

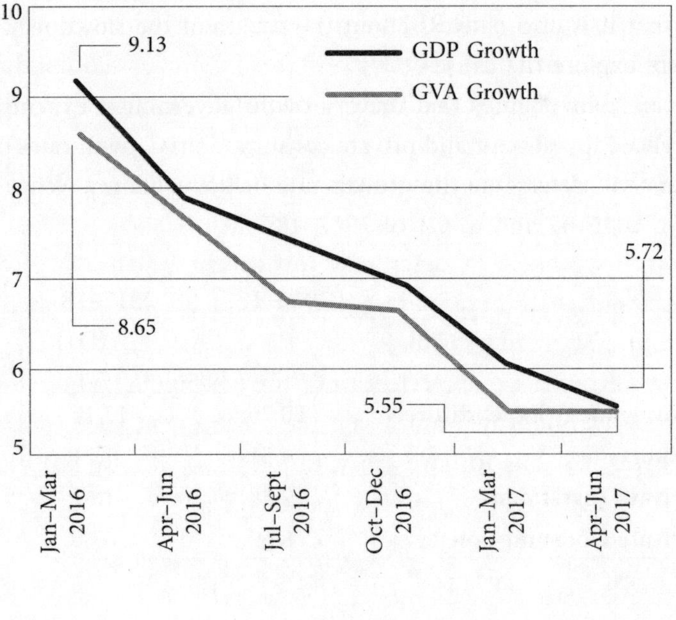

GDP may stabilize at 5.7 per cent or it may decline further in Q2 of 2017–18 (July–September). The effects of demonetisation have not yet dissipated completely. GST, a good idea, was translated into a flawed law that suffered from bad and hurried implementation, and affected many industries in the manufacturing sector. Floods have disrupted normal activity in many parts of India for several weeks.

Empty Boast

In 2016, China's economy grew at 6.7 per cent; in 2016–17, India's economy grew at 7.1 per cent. The size of China's economy is $11,200 billion, India's economy is $2,300 billion. Even if China's economy grew at a rate lower than India's in any year, the value of the domestic product that China added that year would be several times more than what India added in the same year. No country, including China, took our boast seriously; it is, therefore, prudent to be modest.

Every economist has agreed that India's economic growth has slowed down. The CEA has candidly admitted the fact, only his government is in denial! If a government is in denial about the slowdown, it is fair to conclude that it is also clueless about the causes of the slowdown. This column will explore the causes.

There are four engines that drive growth: government expenditure, exports, private investment and private consumption. Growth rates of the four drivers will determine the growth rate of the economy. What were the rates in 2016–17 and in Q1 of 2017–18?

	2016–17	**2017–18**
		(Q1) *(Growth rates, per cent)*
Government Expenditure	20.76	17.17
Exports	4.51	1.21
Private Investment	2.38	1.61
Private Consumption	8.69	6.66

The Table speaks for itself. The government has clutched at the straw of 'spending its way to prosperity'. At the end of July 2017, the government had exhausted 92.4 per cent of the annual target of fiscal deficit. It cannot go much further unless there is an unexpected surge in revenues or it abandons fiscal prudence. The first is not likely and the second is not advised. So, government expenditure would have to be moderated between now and March 2018. The engine can run but only at a steady speed.

Three Engines Sputtering

Exports no longer drive growth. In the 10 years of the UPA government, exports rose to $314 billion in 2013–14, registering a Compound Annual Growth Rate (CAGR) of 17.3 per cent. In the last three years under the NDA government, exports have remained far below the peak: $310 billion, $262 billion and $276 billion. Mr Swaminathan Aiyar has pointed out that no country has achieved a GDP growth of 7 per cent or more if its exports had not grown at 15 per cent a year.

Private investment is also not driving growth. In the last three years, GFCF as a percentage of GDP has been 31.34, 30.92 and 29.55 per cent—well below the peak of 34.31 per cent achieved in 2011–12. Another indicator of private investment is growth of credit to industry. That has been negative for every month since October 2016. The worst hit are medium enterprises where the bulk of the jobs are. Outstanding credit to medium enterprises *declined* from ₹119,268 crore in July 2015 to ₹100,542 crore in July 2017—a shrinkage of 16 per cent! (Yet government wants us to believe that jobs are being created in the industrial sector!)

The IIP rings a bell every month, but no one seems to care or even understand. In April–July 2017, overall IIP grew by a mere 1.7 per cent and manufacturing IIP grew by 1.3 per cent. The July numbers were abysmal: overall 1.2 per cent and manufacturing 0.1 per cent.

And, like the proverbial last straw, growth of private consumption has declined. It slowed down to 6.7 per cent, year on year, in April–July 2017. According to the latest RBI survey, the Current Situation Index fell to 96.8 in June from 100 in May 2017, 'slipping into the pessimistic zone with sentiment showing deterioration across all parameters'. The survey found that while urban sentiment has been subdued, the mood in rural areas has also begun to sour.

Mortal Wounds

All this when the global economy is recovering, crude oil prices are still low, negative or low interest rates in developed economies are pushing funds into India, the exchange rate is stable and inflation is low. Instead of capitalizing on the opportunity, the government inflicted mortal wounds on the economy through demonetisation and a flawed and hastily implemented GST. And to cover up its utter incompetence, the government has inflicted another deep wound by arming tax authorities with draconian powers and unleashing (what every businessperson will privately tell you is) tax terrorism.

Yet, there is no sign of worry on the faces of the prime minister, finance minister and the new industry minister. Journalists who have access to the Prime Minister's Office (PMO) tell us that the PMO is, in fact, worried. The only indication of the worry was the sacking of three ministers connected with jobs and labour (Micro, Small & Medium Enterprises [MSME], Labour and Skill Development) and the transfer of the fourth (Industry).

A clueless government cannot address the causes of the slowdown. Meanwhile, ill-advised measures like demonetisation, flawed GST and tax terrorism will haunt the economy.

SUMMER OF 2014 TO AUTUMN OF 2017

1 October 2017

I did not set the cat among the pigeons. In fact, my grievance was that nothing that more knowledgeable persons (leave aside my views) wrote or said seemed to have any effect on the government and its management of the economy. A course correction was not effected or even hinted at. On the contrary, the government steadfastly and stubbornly maintained that 'God is in heaven and all's well with the world'.

Quite unexpectedly, Mr Yashwant Sinha wrote a centre page article in *The Indian Express* on 27 September 2017. I did not rush to endorse him, I simply pointed out that Mr Sinha had said the same things that many others and I had been saying for 15 months.

Mr Sinha Agrees

Let's look at the main points of Mr Sinha's article (and how they coincided with the views I had expressed in my columns on the dates mentioned below):

- that the BJP/NDA government got an unprecedented oil bonanza that was wasted (14 January 2016)
- that private investment has shrunk as never before in two decades (15 January 2017)

- that industrial production has all but collapsed (11 June 2017)
- that exports have dwindled (1 January 2017)
- that demonetisation has proved to be an unmitigated disaster (3 September 2017)
- that a badly conceived and poorly implemented GST has played havoc with businesses and sunk many of them (2 July 2017)
- that countless millions have lost their jobs with hardly any new opportunities coming the way of the new entrants to the labour market (9 April 2017)
- that the growth rate of 5.7 per cent is actually 3.7 per cent or less

Naturally, the government is red-faced and livid and is pulling out all the stops to heap ridicule and abuse.

The Promise Belied

The summer of 2014 held great promise. The BJP was the first party in 30 years to form a government with an absolute majority. It inherited an economy that had accelerated from 5.5 per cent in 2012–13 to 6.4 per cent in 2013–14 (the government's numbers). Inflation had begun a steady decline from 10.5 per cent in September 2013 (thanks to breaching the fiscal deficit and expenditure limits) to 5.77 per cent in June 2014. The current account deficit (CAD) had been contained at 0.24 per cent in the quarter January–March 2014. The stage had been set for bold structural reforms. The so-called 'legacy' problems is a fake argument. Every government will inherit some issues and it is expected that the government will address them.

Fast forward 40 months.

The autumn of 2017 presents a bleak picture. Economic growth decelerated to 5.7 per cent in April–June 2017; CAD climbed up to 2.4 per cent in that quarter; industrial production shrunk by 0.17 per cent in June and grew by a paltry 1.2 per cent in July; and an estimated 1.5 million jobs were lost between January and April 2017.

How did we go from the great expectations of the summer of 2014 to the disappointing situation of the autumn of 2017? We cannot blame global economic conditions because they have been benign. Actually, according to the IMF, after 3.2 per cent growth in 2016, the global economy is poised to grow at 3.6 per cent in 2017 and 3.7 per cent in 2018. Besides, crude oil prices remain low at $58.30 per barrel.

It is pointless listing the causes once again. Let me examine the deeper reasons behind the apparent incapability of the government to tackle the causative factors.

The Deeper Reasons

Firstly, the absence of a deliberative and inclusive process of decision-making. All authority is concentrated in the PMO. The model may have worked in Gujarat (which I doubt) but it will certainly not work in a federal set-up and when there are so many ministries and departments, autonomous authorities, regulators, and adjudicatory bodies and courts.

Secondly, the bench strength of the BJP. If talent is available, why saddle a minister with multiple portfolios?

Thirdly, by the accounts we hear, the present Cabinet is not a deliberative body. It is more like the Cabinet of a President that will meekly endorse the decisions taken elsewhere. Example: demonetisation. When a Cabinet does not function as a Cabinet, good ideas will not take root and bad ideas will not be stopped.

Fourthly, the government failed to build a credible economic policy team at the beginning of its term. At any given time, there should be at least half-a-dozen internationally reputed economists in the larger government system. Nor did the government place economist-civil servants in key positions in the administration. The government did not wish to retain Dr Raghuram Rajan and could not retain Dr Arvind Panagariya. While Dr Arvind Subramanian has reluctantly agreed to stay on for one more year, it is anybody's guess if he will actually do so.

Fifthly, there is no accountability. A well-intentioned but failed minister of railways has been made minister of industry and commerce. The engine of exports was sputtering, yet the minister of commerce is the new minister of defence. The redeeming feature is Mr Suresh Prabhu is an honest gentleman and Ms Nirmala Sitharaman's appointment is a blow for women's empowerment and breaks an unjust glass ceiling.

Finally, it is possible to infer that the BJP believes it has forged an election-winning (Uttar Pradesh) and/or deal-making (Bihar) formula and hence it need not worry about performance or outcomes.

I don't really care about the deeper reasons as long as the government will acknowledge the causes of the economic slowdown and address them.

THE REAL WORLD BECKONS THE PM

15 October 2017

I was on a train. There was a notice on the cabin wall detailing the procedure to be followed in an emergency. The first instruction read:

'Take a moment to evaluate the situation. DO NOT PANIC.'

How appropriate to the Indian economic situation!

Much has happened in the last ten days. The most important development is that, for the first time, I detect a sense of nervousness among the government's ministers and spokespersons. I welcome the nervousness, because it might make the government more responsive to well-intentioned criticism.

At the same time, there is the usual bluff and bluster. Mr Yashwant Sinha and Mr Arun Shourie were dismissed as individuals who could not sleep at night if they did not find fault with the government. Before the two veterans were bad-mouthed by the prime minister (without taking their names, of course) their views had been heard by millions of Indians, including BJP cadres, and the message had gone home.

Slowdown vs Recession

The prime minister made a valiant effort to debunk the theory of 'slowdown'. His case was built on the fact that certain sectors of the economy had recorded positive growth and he gave the examples of car sales (12 per cent), sale of commercial vehicles (23 per cent), sale of two-wheelers (14 per cent) and increase in air traffic, air freight and telephone subscribers. The prime minister is right, some sectors are growing—but only very few are—and that is why the economy is witnessing what is called a *slowdown.*

What the prime minister's researchers and speech writers failed to tell him was that if *all* sectors of the economy were not growing, the economy will witness a *recession*, not a slowdown. The difference between a slowdown and a recession should have been obvious.

While some sectors are growing, examples of sectors that have witnessed slower growth or a decline in output are:

- mining and quarrying: (-)0.66 per cent
- manufacturing: 1.17
- construction: 2.0
- agriculture, forestry & fishing: 2.34

Together, these four sectors account for 40 per cent of the economy and that explains the slowdown, now acknowledged by the prime minister's newly-constituted Economic Advisory Council.

Graph Tells Story

Without burdening this column with numbers, let me draw your attention to the graph (see next page). It is for the 13 quarters from April 2014 (the NDA came to power in May 2014) until June 2017 for which data has been published by the CSO/RBI. There are two lines: One line is *Investment* as measured by GFCF as a proportion of GDP in that quarter. The second line is *Credit Growth* in that quarter over credit growth in the corresponding quarter of the previous year.

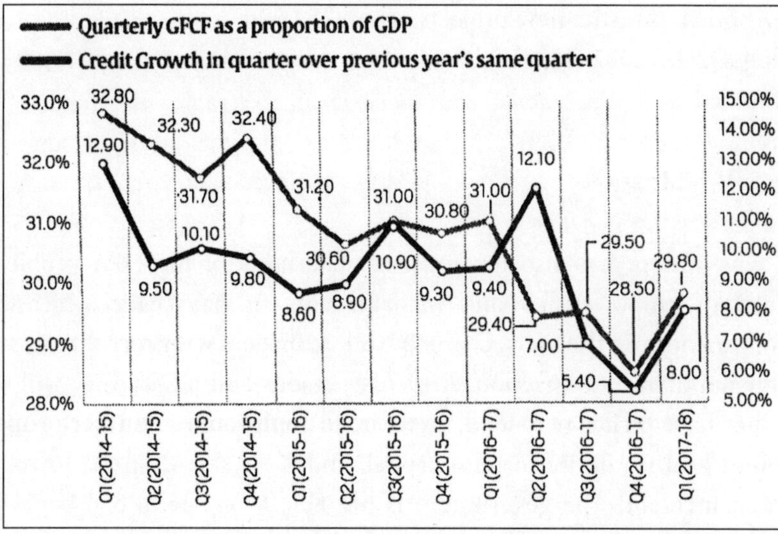

Graph Plotting GFCF (quarterly) and Credit Growth

The two lines, in a very substantial way, tell the story of what the NDA/BJP government has done to the economy. The government has killed the desire to invest in the economy. The chief culprit is the Ministry of Finance. It has made retrospective tax demands for humongous sums. It has brought brutal and draconian amendments to various tax laws as well as made new laws. It has unleashed a raid raj. Assessment Officers have been vested with vast discretion and the power to not disclose reasons. Far from assessments being done with little interface with the assessee, as promised, every case of scrutiny assessment has practically turned out to be an inquisition. Income tax cases are being referred to the Enforcement Directorate for action under the Prevention of Money Laundering Act, 2002 (PMLA). Ask chartered accountants, they will tell you they are busier and earning more, but their clients are swearing under their breath.

The government has not been able to restart stalled projects. In the power sector alone, 30,000 MW of projects are stranded, locking up valuable capital. Bankers have told me that power, telecommunication, steel and construction are the most stressed sectors. There is no scope for new investments in these leading sectors.

Another statistic: new projects worth ₹84,500 crore were announced during Q2 of 2017–18, the lowest in a quarter since this government took office.

The NPA Mess

The government has also made a complete mess of the NPA problem. Instead of empowering bank managements, it has made whimsical appointments and transfers, charged bank managers with corruption, and frightened them into inaction. Ask chairpersons and CEOs, they will tell you they have no desire to lend, no desire to compromise non-performing accounts and no desire to raise capital, and their sole desire is to retire without incident! The government is not able to create a 'bad bank', as it had hinted earlier, to take over the bad loans. Nor is the government able to recapitalize the banks. The bank credit system is in a shambles.

Without reviving private investment and without restarting bank credit, there is little hope of turning the economy around. Over to you, Mr Prime Minister.

IGNORE THIRUVALLUVAR AT YOUR PERIL

29 October 2017

Words speak louder than action. The finance minister was loud and clear so that the message will reach not-too-distant Gujarat.

He said, 'We will provide ₹211,000 crore to recapitalise public sector banks; and we will implement a new programme, BharatMala, on an outlay of ₹535,000 crore and build 34,800 km of roads.' He also said, 'The economy is on strong macroeconomic fundamentals,' and added, almost apologetically, 'And where we have identified the need for a boost, in relation to that we have taken some decisions.' The Secretary, Economic Affairs, chimed in: 'India grew at a very strong pace of 7.5 per cent in the three years of 2014–17.'

If the economy is on strong macroeconomic fundamentals and is growing at 7.5 per cent, it does not require a boost! A boost to such an economy may prove inflationary, push up the fiscal deficit, worsen the current account deficit and so on. Obviously, there is something wrong in the diagnosis.

Wrong Diagnosis

The diagnosis is at variance with that of most economists and with the CSO's numbers. Let's keep the views aside and focus on the numbers. The sequential quarterly growth rates of GDP since January–March 2016 have been 9.1, 7.9, 7.5, 7.0, 6.1 and 5.7 per cent. The economy is, therefore, not growing at 7.5 per cent. It was growing at a brisk rate but was derailed, and it has been decelerating since April 2016. That is the first flaw in the diagnosis.

The second and more serious flaw is not identifying the causes of the deceleration. Saint Thiruvalluvar said:

> *Noi nadi noi muthal nadi athu thanikkum*
> *vai nadi vaippa cheyal*
>
> (Make a careful diagnosis, discover the true cause, think of the proper remedy and apply it effectively)

A careful diagnosis would have revealed that the proximate causes were the sputtering engines of private investment, private consumption and exports. The two decisions announced by the government will have little impact on the sluggish engines of growth.

Recapitalization Not Panacea

Recapitalization of banks is good in itself and I welcome it. Due to write-offs, banks' capital has been reduced. There will be more write-offs as 12 companies have been referred to insolvency resolution and more cases are likely to follow suit. Recapitalization will help banks maintain their capital adequacy ratio. Banks' *capacity* to lend will increase, but that does not mean *lending* will increase.

No entrepreneur believes that the situation today is conducive to start or expand a business. (Notice that the government no longer speaks of 'ease of doing business'!) Unless private investors discover their appetite for making more investment (including investing their own money and borrowing from banks), merely recapitalizing banks will not restart private investment. The paramount need is to boost investment in Small & Medium Enterprises (SMEs). Banks lend to SMEs only about 10 per cent of their credit needs. Recapitalizing banks will make little difference to the dire situation of SMEs.

Besides, there are downsides to the government's proposal. The government will issue bonds, banks will subscribe to the bonds, and the government will invest that money in the same banks as equity! It is a case of 'rob Peter to pay Peter'! As a consequence, the fiscal deficit limit will, in all likelihood, be breached, resulting in its own adverse consequences.

Recapitalization is a half-reform done three years late, as pointed out by the CEA on 25 October 2017. According to the CEA, it has to be accompanied by—I would say preceded by—banking reforms and tough governance standards. Read Part III of his speech. There is no word from the government on these concomitant reforms.

Road Scheme Mere Announcement

The other proposal is to build 34,800 km of roads. This number includes 10,000 km already under the National Highway Development Project. The rest is distributed among economic corridors, feeder routes, efficiency improvement, border roads and coastal roads. There are several steps before work can start on any new road—prepare a Detailed Project Report (DPR) for each road project, get environment clearance, acquire land, bid out the project, tie up financing, fix the toll, etc. No significant part of the 34,800 km is likely to be started or completed in the next 18 months.

There are many other things the government could have done. It could have declared it will never again indulge in reckless adventurism like demonetisation. It could have brought in a group of outside experts to quickly fix the mess created by the hasty implementation of the flawed GST. It could have promised to rescind the draconian amendments made to the tax laws and the excessive powers given to tax officials. It could have promised to rein in the investigative agencies that have struck terror among business persons.

None of the above seems to be of interest to the government. Instead we have *jumlon ki baarish* (a shower of promises). Let's brace ourselves for jobless growth and despondency among the youth.

NOW, RETURN TO GOVERNANCE

17 December 2017

Come to the world of the new normal. The new normal is that elections will be fought not on the performance of the ruling party (of 22 years, in the case of Gujarat) but on an indiscreet remark that will be distorted and blown out of proportion to the weight it deserved.

The New Normal

The new normal is that outrageous allegations can and will be levelled against a former vice president of India, a former prime minister of India, a former chief of army staff, former high commissioners to Pakistan and several former civil servants and, when called out, an apology will be demanded from the former prime minister!

The new normal is that the government's position will become the 'national' position and everyone will be forbidden to hold a view contrary to the 'national' position! (So, believe that demonetisation was good, the design and implementation of GST were perfectly fine, the 'first-ever surgical strike' pulverized Pakistan and the Doklam standoff ended in a decisive victory for India over China.)

The new normal is that every rule will be bent to influence the election—ride on a borrowed seaplane from the Sabarmati waterfront to the Dharoi dam on the last day of campaign or launch a new submarine on polling day.

In the run-up to the parliamentary election in 2014, Mr Narendra Modi had reinvented himself as a moderate politician whose paramount interest was the economic development of India and, in fact, of all the people of India. Many controversial aspects of his brand of governance as chief minister of Gujarat were buried in a brilliantly conceived and imaginatively executed election campaign. The result vindicated the person and the campaign.

That model was turned on its head in the election to the Gujarat Legislature. In a state that the BJP had ruled for 22 years, the Party did not run on its record. The BJP's campaign was a textbook case study of how a well-oiled election machine, bereft of ethics and using unlimited resources, can blur the difference between truth and hype. The Party may still ride to victory.

Heed the Warning Signals

Meanwhile, the economy continues to tank. The fact that the government is celebrating a minor upturn in the growth rate (from 5.7 per cent in Q1 of 2017–18 to 6.3 per cent in Q2) is quite telling. In October 2017, the IIP grew by a paltry 2.2 per cent over the same month a year ago. Manufacturing grew by 2.5 per cent. Inflation continued to rise: retail inflation that was 3.6 per cent in October inched up to 4.9 per cent in November and it was driven by the rise in prices of essential items of consumption. For example, inflation in vegetable prices was 22.5 per cent, up from 7.5 per cent in the previous month. Agriculture recorded a dismal growth rate of 1.7 per cent in the second quarter (July–September) of 2017–18.

The numbers are not likely to get much better in the near term. In July–September 2017, only 246 private sector projects with a total expected investment of ₹43,492 crore were announced. It was the lowest in more than 10 years. Corporate India has neither the appetite nor the money to make new investments. In Q1 and Q2 of the current fiscal year, corporate profits shrunk by 21 per cent and 8.6 per cent, respectively, over the corresponding quarters of 2016–17.

I do not know when the government will engage with the real—and worrisome—issues concerning the economy. On 14 December 2017, the prime minister made an important speech at the annual meeting of FICCI. The headline-grabbing point was that there was an organized loot of the banking system by the previous government! As expected, the lambs in the gathering were silent and some even cheered!

Truth vs Hype about NPAs

Is the NPA problem a case of organized loot? The facts speak for themselves (see Table below):

	2012–13	**2013–14**	**2014–15**	**2015–16**	**2016–17**
Public Sector Banks Gross NPA (in crore rupees)	155,890	216,739	267,065	502,068	641,057
Gross NPA Ratio (in per cent)	3.84	4.72	5.43	9.83	12.47

At the end of March 2014, ₹216,739 crore of loans were *non-performing*. That means that the remaining loans were *performing* and interest and instalments of the principal were being paid regularly. Why did the performing loans become non-performing? Why did the NPAs of private sector banks also increase nearly fourfold from ₹19,986 crore to ₹73,842 crore? The answer is the downturn in the domestic economy and the deterioration in the external environment that affected exports. Of course, there was also malfeasance by some borrowers.

Besides, there is another question that the government has shied away from answering. How much of the NPA amount at the end of March 2017 were loans given *after* the NDA took office in May 2014? Further, if the charge of organized loot is correct, why did the banks (and the government) write off, in the period 2014–15 to 2016–17, a sum of ₹188,287 crore of the loans to defaulters?

I hope that after the unedifying spectacle of the election campaign in Gujarat, we can return to a debate on the economy, but the debate cannot start on a false note and an unsubstantiated charge. As candidate Bill Clinton said, 'It's the economy, stupid' and the economy is still in the sick ward.

BUDGET

The Budget is the defining event of the annual economic calendar. I had taken great pains to list the Do's and Don'ts in the Budget for 2017–18 in the vain hope that the finance minister would accept at least some of the suggestions. He did the exact opposite! My conclusion was that, as late as January 2017, the government had not woken up to the fact that the growth rate of the economy had begun to slide from the middle of 2016. An opportunity to arrest the slide was missed and the country is paying the price.

IT IS A BALLOON, IT IS A KITE!

22 January 2017

It is the Budget season. The good, bad and ugly (ideas) will be on display. One idea that is in the realm of speculation is Universal Basic Income (UBI). The CEA has promised a detailed analysis of the subject in the Economic Survey that will be presented to Parliament on the eve of the Budget. However, there is no word yet from the government. Usually voluble ministers have been careful not to utter a word on the subject.

UBI is not a novel idea. Countries that have a comprehensive social security scheme provide cash payment as well as food coupons to persons entitled to receive social security benefits (too poor, unemployed, disabled, aged). In India, there is no comprehensive social security scheme. We have the Mahatma Gandhi National Rural Employment Guarantee Scheme (MGNREGS) that bears a similarity to UBI. The Mahatma Gandhi National Rural Employment Guarantee Act (MGNREGA) guarantees work on demand and pays a wage per day that is equivalent to the prevailing wage of a farm labourer.

If MGNREGA is implemented in letter and spirit, it will provide work and wages for 100 days in a year at the currently notified wage that, on average, is ₹195 per day. A working person can receive up to ₹19,500 per year. That amount will supplement any other income of the person.

Antidote to Poverty

Under UBI, the State will transfer a certain amount to every person to supplement his/her income so that the total income of the person reached a certain threshold. Not many countries have UBI. Recently, Switzerland, with a per capita income of $79,578, rejected a proposal in a referendum to grant UBI. Finland, with a per capita income of $45,133, has announced a pilot project where a small number of people will receive a modest amount of $595 per month. Switzerland and Finland are among the richest countries in the world.

We may presume that UBI is meant to address the problem of poverty. The idea is that an income transfer will help improve outcomes by assuring poor people, or those at the edge of poverty, a certain level of basic consumption, so that they may focus on improving their economic status. As a principle of equity, it is unexceptionable and I support the idea.

However, I must reiterate my firm belief that the best antidote to poverty is economic growth. Thanks to the higher rate of growth since 1991, India's poverty headcount ratio has halved and the number of poor people in the country has fallen by about a third. Between 2004 and 2014 (the period under the UPA), 140 million people were lifted out of poverty. Even the welfare schemes became feasible because tax revenues increased in the years of high economic growth.

The Design is Crucial

The UBI idea raises a set of interrelated questions:

- Will UBI replace other schemes where benefits are gradually being converted into direct cash transfers?
- Will the coverage be 'universal' as the name suggests or will there be a target population?
- Will the transfer be unconditional or will conditions apply?
- What is the level of income that can be considered 'basic'?
- How will the resources for the scheme be raised?

The most challenging questions are, what is the level of income that can be considered as 'basic' to enable a person to meet his basic consumption requirements and what will UBI cost? Suppose we take the measure of the poverty line which is, on average, ₹40 per day (₹32 in rural areas and ₹47 in urban areas). Every person should be assured of an income of about ₹14,000 per year or ₹1,200 per month. That is a modest and reasonable amount. Assume that 25 per cent of the population (330 million) would need a transfer of ₹14,000, another 25 per cent (330 million) would need a transfer of ₹7,000 and the remaining would require nothing, the cost would be ₹693,000 crore per year or 35 per cent of the expenditure budget for 2016–17—obviously beyond the present capacity of the government. Even if we halve the UBI amount or halve the number of beneficiaries, it will cost ₹346,500 crore per year.

Funding UBI

To find the resources, assume that we can eliminate all the current subsidies to the non-poor. The Economic Survey 2015–16 estimated that about ₹100,000 crore worth of subsidies were accruing to the non-poor. Even if we can free up this fiscal space, it would not be sufficient to meet the UBI bill. Can more fiscal space be created? There is talk about revenues foregone, but once you look below the surface, you will realize that most of these are difficult to dismantle. Many of the 'revenues foregone' are meant to achieve specific policy objectives and withdrawing them would mean discarding the policy objectives such as Special Economic Zones (SEZs), accelerated depreciation, investments in specified infrastructure, etc. We cannot assume that getting rid of them to pay for UBI would be more beneficial to the economy or the people.

Sadly, it appears that there is an intent to push through the idea without adequate thought or discussion. The buzz is that UBI is desperately needed as an antidote to the misery caused by demonetisation.

If there is not a carefully designed UBI and if it is not feasible to create enough fiscal space to fund UBI, what we may get is another feel-good *jumla* (promise) that will have negligible impact on the problem of poverty while making the fiscal situation precarious. The irony is that the idea, if accepted, will be implemented by a party/government that came to power promising development and jobs, but which seems to have given up on that agenda.

NAVIGATING THROUGH THE DO'S AND DON'TS

29 January 2017

Every budget is determined by the context and the context is determined by the circumstances—economic, political and the year in the term of the government. Budget 2017–18 will be the fourth budget of the NDA government (one more remains) and it will be presented when, according to the RBI and the CSO, the economy is slowing down. The political circumstance is that the Budget will be presented when the election process is under way in five states, including the prize state of Uttar Pradesh.

The Red Lines

At this point in its term, a government cannot make too many new promises: there will not be enough time to deliver tangible outcomes on any new promise and the time that remains has to be used to deliver on the old promises. That's the first *red* line.

The outlook for the world's economy is uncertain. Two developments are likely: the US government may turn against free trade and overseas investments by American companies and the US Fed may raise domestic interest rates. Since November 2016, foreign capital has been flowing out of India. The Budget must not send any signal that will accelerate the outflow. Hence, it has to remain steadfast on the path of fiscal consolidation (FD < 3 per cent), containing the CAD (< 1.5 per cent), and price stability (CPI < 4 per cent). That's the second *red* line.

The government's assessment of the security situation is bleak and pessimistic. The new Chief of Army Staff has talked of being prepared for a two-front war (leaving us wondering why he said that). The government is on a massive arms-buying spree and the bills must be paid in 2017–18 and subsequent years. The Budget must provide for a very large increase in the defence budget, reducing the space for other expenditure. That's the third *red* line.

Private investment has practically dried up. Credit growth is at its lowest level in several decades. Exports are languishing. Demonetisation has hit private consumption. The only engine left to the government is government expenditure. If government increases its capital expenditure, less money will be available for welfare programmes. That's the fourth *red* line.

Corporates expect a sharp cut in corporate tax as a reward for not vocally protesting a disruptive action like demonetisation and widespread excesses by tax officials in the name of tax law enforcement. Individuals expect a cut in personal income tax rates as recompense for the misery caused by demonetisation and increased indirect taxes. The government will look foolish if, after cutting tax rates, the budget projects aggressive tax revenue targets. That's the fifth *red* line.

How will the finance minister navigate his way among these red lines? And how will he find the revenues for the new paths that the prime minister and the BJP seem to want to cut? We may take note of the balloons that have been floated in recent weeks:

- Loan waiver for farmers
- UBI
- Cut in corporate tax rates
- Banking Cash Transaction Tax (BCTT)

I shall now offer my unsolicited advice to the finance minister. I think the government, having shot itself in the foot by demonetisation, should quietly accept that growth in 2017–18 and 2018–19 will be between 6 and 7 per cent, and that is not a rate of growth that should be scoffed at. The government must firmly reject policy advice based on an exaggerated estimate of the growth rate. Once this issue is settled, it is fairly easy to identify the Do's and Don'ts for the finance minister.

The Do's

- The N.K. Singh Committee is reported to have carved out a few exceptions to the fiscal deficit limit of 3 per cent. In my view, the only justifiable exception is when there is a declared war. Stick to the target of 3 per cent in 2017–18.
- Promote private investment. Hold talks individually with business houses and entrepreneurs and help them at every step until the project has achieved Commercial Operation Date. Target 50 major projects in 2017–18.
- Sell loss-making public sector enterprises (PSEs) and divest the government's stake up to 100 per cent in non-core PSEs.
- Pass the GST Bills and implement GST no later than 1 October 2017. Aim at a broad tax base than at a high tax rate. Cut wasteful government expenditure and use the savings to compensate the states for any revenue shortfall.
- Update the Direct Taxes Code (DTC) and pass it. It is the best answer to tax rate and tax evasion conundrums.

And the Don'ts

- Do not cut direct tax rates. Instead, cut indirect tax rates (especially service tax and excise duties on petroleum products that have given you a 'sugar high' of revenue collection) to stimulate aggregate demand.
- Do not announce UBI. If you must, announce a pilot scheme and learn as you go forward. That's how the Direct Benefit Transfer (DBT) and Aadhaar became the success they have.
- Do not introduce BCTT. Instead, amend the Income-Tax Act to expand

the list of transactions that mandatorily require non-cash payments. Don't meddle with the right of the people to use cash for normal, small transactions.

- Do not give up on reforms. Leave 'welfarism' to the states.
- Do not blame the UPA for the current economic situation. (The UPA delivered average growth of 7.5 per cent over 10 years and lifted 140 million people out of poverty.) You have been in charge for 32 months.

MUDDLING THROUGH ANOTHER BUDGET, ANOTHER YEAR

5 February 2017

Budget day has come and gone. Millions of words have been spoken and written since 1 February 2017. Not many will remember the numbers or the artful phrases (there was none in this edition) or the flashes of poetry (who were the poets?). What will remain is the question—did the Budget leave the average citizen with the belief that the fundamental issues are being or will be addressed? Let me go straight to the heart of the matter.

Many people are poor. They have little or no income. They—or their children—do not have jobs. Everything else follows: poor housing, poor health, no access to healthcare, little education, discrimination and neglect, vulnerability, and denial of opportunity. Most children of the middle class also seek jobs but cannot find them. The proven antidote to poverty and joblessness is rapid economic growth. It may be an old cliché, but it is absolutely true that a rising tide will lift all (or nearly all) boats.

After reading the 37-page, 184-paragraph Budget speech, I am left with the impression that India will not return to the path of high growth in 2017–18 or even in 2018–19.

A Dismal Record

The government has admitted that private investment is in the doldrums. The government is embarrassed by the fact that, in 2015–16, only 150,000 jobs were created. This is the twin challenge.

GFCF is a widely used measure of investment, including private investment. According to the Economic Survey, growth of GFCF in the last three financial years was:

2014–15	4.9 per cent
2015–16	3.9 per cent
2016–17	(-) 0.2 per cent

As for job creation, the best result under the NDA government was 150,000 jobs in 2015–16—a far shot from the promise of creating two crore jobs a year.

Obvious Measures

What should the government have done? Here is a list of measures that were obvious, but not taken:

1. **Boost aggregate demand:** The tried, tested and best way to increase aggregate demand is to cut indirect taxes that are paid by all consumers of goods and services—poor, middle class and rich. If indirect taxes are cut, many millions of consumers will get immediate monetary relief. Producers of goods and services will benefit by increased sales. New capacities and new jobs will be created. I advocated this option in the list of do's in my column of 29 January 2017 titled 'Navigating Through the Do's and Don'ts'. To my disappointment, the Budget rejected this option and chose the one that I had included in the list of don'ts—cutting direct taxes!
2. **Lend a helping hand to MSMEs:** Micro, small and medium enterprises are the low-cost producers and job-creators. The demand contraction has hurt them badly. Demonetisation has forced nearly 80 per cent

of MSMEs to close down. Most MSMEs are not companies; they are proprietorships or partnerships. 597,000 to 694,000 companies file income-tax returns and, among them, only 285,000 make profits. According to the Budget speech, 96 per cent of such companies will qualify as MSMEs. Cutting the corporate tax rate for MSMEs (from 30 to 25 per cent) will therefore benefit only about 270,000 companies. If the taxable income is modest, the benefit too will be modest. It will do nothing to increase sales or create new jobs. On the other hand, if excise duties and service tax had been cut, it would have boosted demand and revived many MSMEs that had shut down. That opportunity was missed.

3. **Energize the Project Monitoring Group (PMG):** Every business house and every major entrepreneur has at least one project that is stalled or stranded. If a businessperson has one stalled project in his basket, he will be loath to make a new investment. We have not seen or heard from the PMG in a long time.

The Unwanted Interruption

4. **Accept that demonetisation was a very disruptive step:** The worst affected were farmers, farm labour, manual workers, the self-employed, artisans and MSMEs. Crores of rupees were lost in terms of wages, incomes, operating losses and capital losses. The Budget should have provided them some form of compensation. Farmers should have been compensated through higher MSPs. Cut in indirect taxes (or reduction in power tariff for a limited period) would have brought immediate relief to all. The other option was an increase in minimum wages across all sectors. It is a pity that none of these options was explored.
5. **Lend more:** Thanks to NPAs, investors are ineligible or unwilling to borrow and banks are unable to lend. Hence, credit growth to all industries is at an all-time low, and turned negative in October 2016. Take a look at the NPA situation of public sector banks:

As on	Gross NPA ratio (Per cent of Gross Advances)
31-3-2014	4.5
31-3-2015	4.6
31-3-2016	7.8
31-12-2016	9.1

Loan accounts that were 'performing' as on 31 March 2014 have become 'non-performing' under the NDA government, thanks to the deteriorating economic situation. The government can no longer airily dismiss the problem as a 'legacy' issue. To make matters worse, the Budget provided a measly ₹10,000 crore to recapitalize public sector banks, leaving the banks to fend for themselves. Unless the government finds solutions, more woes are in store for the banks and industry, even while credit growth will remain tepid.

Budget 2017–18 will be remembered not for any bold measure but because it did not do great damage to the economy. India will muddle through another year of hopes belied and aspirations unfulfilled.

WANTED EXPANSION, GOT CONTRACTION

12 February 2017

A budget is contextual. When 2017 dawned, some things were abundantly clear. Firstly, the external environment was no longer benign (rising oil prices and rising protectionism). Secondly, the growth rate of the Indian economy was slowing down (as in many countries of the world). Thirdly, while the Indian economy was growing, few jobs were being created. Fourthly, there was acute distress in the farm sector. Fifthly, three of the four engines of growth (private investment, private consumption and exports) were sputtering. Sixthly, demonetisation was a terrible disruption of the India growth story.

The context ought to have set the overall objectives of Budget 2017–18. Those objectives ought to have been reflected in the finance minister's Budget speech, the numbers in the Budget documents and the provisions of the Finance Bill. Sadly, nothing was evident from the Budget speech. Nor did the finance minister spell out the objectives in his numerous post-Budget interviews to the media.

Context Sets Goals

Under UPA I (2004–09), we chased growth to lift the growth rate from the average of 5.9 per cent recorded during the Atal Bihari Vajpayee government (1999–2004). Beginning September 2008 and until 2012

(UPA II), the goal was to counter the consequences of the international financial crisis (September 2008) and maintain growth. After August 2012, the aim was to pull back the economy from the deviations and renew the commitment to fiscal consolidation. In 2012–13 and 2013–14, the objective was to deliver on fiscal consolidation, inflation control and growth. Such an overarching goal is absent in Budget 2017–18.

One thing is clear: demonetisation hangs like a dark cloud over the government and its exertions. The government wants to reboot the economy but it does not know what risks it can take. For an economy that is slowing down perceptibly, and not creating sufficient jobs, the textbook prescription is to increase public expenditure. The finance minister claimed that he had done that and pointed to a rise in total expenditure from ₹2,014,407 crore in 2016–17 (RE) to ₹2,146,735 crore in 2017–18 (BE). That is impressive—but only until you convert all expenditure numbers into percentage of GDP.

The Contraction

When all economists were agreed and the Economic Survey had recommended an increase in government expenditure, the government has chosen to reduce its expenditure as a proportion of GDP! Not only total expenditure, but expenditure under crucial heads has *declined* as a percentage of GDP in the Budget for 2017–18 (see Table below).

(as a per cent of GDP) (GDP for 2017–18 projected at 16,847,455 crore)			
Head	**2015–16**	**2016–17 (RE)**	**2017–18 (BE)**
Total Expenditure	13.09	13.36	12.74
National Education Mission	0.20	0.19	0.18
MGNREGS	0.27	0.32	0.28
Pradhan Mantri Gram Sadak Yojna (PMGSY)	0.13	0.13	0.11

(Continued on p. 97)

(Continued from p. 96)

Fertiliser Subsidy	0.53	0.46	0.42
Food Subsidy	1.02	0.90	0.86
Interest Subsidy on Farm Loans	0.10	0.09	0.09
National Social Assistance Programme (NSAP)	0.06	0.06	0.06
Mid Day Meal Scheme	0.07	0.06	0.06

Even in a crucial area like Defence capital expenditure, there will be a decline in expenditure. The capital outlay on Defence Services (Army, Navy and Air Force) was the following:

2015–16	₹71,674 crore
2016–17 BE	₹78,586 crore
2016–17 RE	₹71,515 crore
2017–18 BE	₹78,078 crore

The conclusions are obvious. The Defence Ministry is not expected to spend the amount allocated to it in 2016–17 for capital expenditure. It will fall short by ₹7,071 crore, nearly 9 per cent of the allocation. Hence, the finance minister has cut the Budget allocation for 2017–18 from ₹78,586 crore to ₹78,078 crore. Since that would not look 'nice', he has puffed up the number by adding ₹8,364 crore by the simple expedient of showing sums allocated to the heads of Defence Ordnance Factories, R&D and Directorate General of Quality Assurance (DGQA) under 'Capital Outlay on Defence Services'!

Also, if you look at the table (at the top), you will be alarmed to find that the allocation (as a per cent of GDP) remains the same for 2016–17 RE and 2017–18 BE for crucial programmes such as Interest Subsidy on Farm Loans, National Social Assistance Programme or NSAP (old age pensions) and Mid Day Meal Scheme. Allowing for rise in the number of beneficiaries and rise in cost in the case of midday meals, the effect of such 'constant' allocation may actually turn out to be a 'reduction'.

Fear Haunts Government

Why did the government, against all advice, adopt a contractionary strategy? The ostensible reason is 'to meet the fiscal deficit target', but even after contraction the target has not been met. It has been set at 3.2 per cent in 2017–18 BE when it should have been set at 3.0 per cent. It is obvious that

- the government fears that it has overestimated the GDP for 2017–18; or
- the government's revenue projections are aggressive and may not be achieved; or
- the government's estimates of expenditure are understated; or
- all of the above.

Will the strategy work? Will it boost economic activity and deliver growth of over 7 per cent? Will it attract private investment? Will it create jobs? I doubt it.

The government should have adopted an expansionary strategy coupled with bold and broad reforms. It should have attempted a more ambitious disinvestment programme. It should have implemented the recommendations of the Expenditure Reforms Committee (appointed by it) and cut wasteful expenditure and expenditure that have yielded no results. Fear haunts the government. It seems to have given up on bold reforms.

POLITICS

In a developing country, economics should drive politics. Alas, in India it is politics that drives economics. Indian politics remained divisive and ugly through 2017. I wrote three successive columns on 'That Sinking Feeling'. The last column in this section reflects the hope that our politics will become inclusive and worthy of the great country that we aspire to be. I continue to nurture that hope.

THE RISE AND FALL OF THE AIADMK

19 February 2017

De mortuis nil nisi bonum (Of the dead say nothing but the good). The best I can do is to say nothing uncharitable about Jayalalithaa the person, but simply recount the events of the last 25 years. M.G. Ramachandran (MGR) broke with his party, Dravida Munnetra Kazhagam (DMK), in 1972, and founded the All India Anna Dravida Munnetra Kazhagam (AIADMK). He was elected as the chief minister in 1977, 1980 and 1984 and was undefeated until his death. He picked Jayalalithaa and groomed her. After MGR's death, the party split, lost the election in 1989, but reunited under the leadership of Jayalalithaa. Soon, Jayalalithaa gained absolute control of the party and recast it as a loyal congregation that worshipped her as a deity.

Took Perilous Path

Jayalalithaa was first elected as chief minister in 1991. During her first term (1991–96), she and her cohorts (Ms V.K. Sasikala and her group) embarked upon a perilous course to amass wealth by corrupt and illegal means. Although Jayalalithaa was elected thrice subsequently (2001, 2011 and 2016) and she enjoyed the support of a large proportion of the electorate until her death, the reputation of the AIADMK was steadily and irretrievably damaged. It was not the same party that was founded by MGR.

The charges of corruption in the disproportionate assets (DA) case against Jayalalithaa and others before the Supreme Court pertained to the period 1991–96. In Jayalalithaa's second and third terms in office, most other cases against her collapsed one after another. The DA case survived, as did a few other cases. Neither the cases nor the legal setbacks deterred Ms Sasikala and her group. They accumulated more wealth in the second and third terms as well. What defied comprehension was how a person as intelligent as Jayalalithaa did not realize that she was being pushed into a deep hole out of which she could never emerge unscathed. While Jayalalithaa enjoyed the goodwill of large sections of the people, the same sections had silently turned against Ms Sasikala and her group. Few political observers had noticed this duality in the attitude of the people.

Jayalalithaa died on 5 December 2016. On 14 February 2017, the Supreme Court upheld the judgement of the trial court in the DA case and ordered Ms Sasikala and two others to serve the sentence imposed on them. Jayalalithaa was spared the ignominy of going to prison. The two factions of the AIADMK do not seem to have grasped the gravity and import of the judgement. One faction is 'celebrating' the judgement, seemingly oblivious to the fact that Jayalalithaa was also found guilty! The other faction is 'dismissive' of the judgement notwithstanding that the leader they had elected a few days before will spend the next four years in a prison! The people of Tamil Nadu, however, cannot be uncaring or forgiving.

Fierce Ambition

Now, after Jayalalithaa's death, the AIADMK is poised to undergo another self-destructing transformation. There was a fragile arrangement for a few days—Ms Sasikala as general secretary of the party and Mr O. Panneerselvam as chief minister—but, as predicted, the arrangement broke down in the face of the fierce ambition of Ms Sasikala and her family. Her goal was not control of the party alone, her goal was control of the government.

It was an audacious move, but it was of a piece with the impudence and audacity displayed by Ms Sasikala's group since 1996. The people's hostility towards Ms Sasikala erupted in the open only after she bulldozed her way to become general secretary of the party and, within a few days, again bulldozed her way to be elected leader of the AIADMK legislature party. Social media exploded in her face, but Ms Sasikala did not seem to notice or, worse, did not seem to care.

The AIADMK first suffered a horizontal split. The vast majority of the people, especially the poorer classes and women, were outspoken in their opposition to her. The rank and file of the party was disillusioned and became sullen and inactive. It was only the MLAs and party office-bearers who obediently paid tribute to Ms Sasikala and behaved like her vassals.

The End Game

Now, the AIADMK could face a vertical split too. If the legislators cannot or will not shake off the stranglehold of Ms Sasikala, even if the government under the new leader, Mr E.K. Palaniswami, is able to prove its majority, the disconnect between the people and the party/government will deepen.

The portents are not encouraging. Just before she left for Bengaluru to begin her prison term, Ms Sasikala readmitted two of her nephews into the party (they had been expelled by Jayalalithaa) and appointed one of them (Mr Dhinakaran) as the deputy general secretary to run the party in her absence. It is astonishing that Ms Sasikala believes that she can run the party and the government from prison through her proxies for the next four years! Her latest moves have sealed the disconnect between her and the people of Tamil Nadu. Ms Sasikala is perhaps the most reviled public figure in Tamil Nadu today.

In its forty-fourth year, the AIADMK seems to be hurtling towards its demise. It is a cruel twist of fate that a party founded on the plank of fighting corruption will be buried by the corruption of its third (and last?) supreme leader.

THE PEOPLE HAVE VOTED; NOW, WE HOPE

12 March 2017

I was permitted by the editors to hold back this column for a day to take into account the results of the five state elections. That was necessary. It was also a wise decision.

There is no doubt whatsoever that the victories in Uttar Pradesh and Uttarakhand have reconfirmed that Mr Narendra Modi is the most dominant political leader in the country today. The scale of the BJP's victory in these two states is unprecedented and mind-boggling. No one had been prepared for this—until the exit polls put out these numbers. I have to admit that, this time, the pollsters got it right and the election experts (including Mr Prashant Kishor's team) got it wrong, reversing the Bihar experience!

Punjab also has delivered a clear verdict in favour of the Amarinder Singh-led Congress. Mr Rahul Gandhi's decision to name Mr Amarinder Singh as the candidate for chief minister dispelled all doubts and gave the voters a recognizable name in which they could repose their faith after 10 years of misgovernance.

As I sign off this column at 4 p.m. on 11 March 2017, Manipur and Goa seem to have delivered mixed verdicts. Small states with small-sized legislatures electing 'hung' houses do not augur well for good governance in those states.

Carefully Crafted Strategy

The man of the moment is Mr Narendra Modi. He has convincingly demonstrated that his appeal is pan-Indian. It extends from Gujarat and Goa to Assam and Manipur. After slipping badly in Bihar, he has regained his prime position as a master of communication. The text of his message in 2014 was development; in 2017, he has cleverly altered the text to development +, and the debate has to now focus on that elusive and indefinable element that he has added to the text of his message. The *sab* in *Sabka Saath, Sabka Vikas* has been subtly altered to include certain sections of the people and exclude others.

Uttar Pradesh was the laboratory to try the new, altered message. It was the perfect setting. Long divided and exploited on caste lines, with religious animosity just under the surface, the BJP tried to 'Hinduise' the castes and set them apart from the non-Hindu sections of the people (which in the case of Uttar Pradesh meant the Muslims). The messaging was subtle: land for *kabristan* (burial site), but equal land for *shamshan* (cremation ground) too. Electricity for Eid, but electricity for Diwali too. A fact-check revealed that there was no instance of discrimination as insinuated, but facts are not important when latent prejudices and animosities are brought to the surface. The BJP's messaging found its target, the master communicator was at his best, and the results have proved that the BJP's strategists were right.

Uttar Pradesh has a population as large as Brazil's. The size of the Muslim population in Uttar Pradesh is larger than the population of many overwhelmingly Islamic countries. Yet, the BJP claimed that it could not find a single eligible person among Muslims that it could field as a candidate in any of the 403 seats! The message was clear: Muslims will not vote for us or support us, so we are not required to field Muslims or support Muslims. The message was not so much directed towards the Muslims as it was to the castes that were to be brought under the project of 'Hinduisation'.

I must also acknowledge that Mr Narendra Modi, after nearly three years as prime minister, remains an indefatigable campaigner. He is, at his core, a *pracharak* and he loves *prachar* (propaganda). He set aside convention and conventional wisdom to campaign for three full days in his constituency, Varanasi. Since he has delivered an unparalleled result, I suppose no one is complaining!

Brace for the Consequences

The results of the five state elections will have consequences.

On the eve of the Bihar election I had said that 'win or lose, the BJP could move in either direction'. I had hoped that the BJP would pause, take stock, pull back and steer the country on the path of development. The BJP government did not. It pressed on with its agenda of hyper-nationalism. Self-appointed commissars asserted themselves in public spaces, universities and colleges (and recently even on the streets of Kochi). Dalits, religious minorities, young girls, women, gays, NGOs, social activists, journalists, academics and writers live in fear, in different degrees of course, but nonetheless fear. As a result of these distractions, the government has taken its eyes off the ball (of economy).

The so-called surgical strike across the Line of Control (LoC), the hard, militarist policy in the Kashmir Valley, and demonetisation were major disruptions. I admit that large sections of the people are willing to believe the prime minister that these disruptive policies will be good in the long run and I am, perhaps, in a minority. Nevertheless, the fact is that the growth rate of the economy measured by GVA (favoured by the government) has slowed down perceptibly since Q4 of 2015–16. The growth rates of GVA in the last four quarters (that is calendar 2016) were: 7.83, 6.89, 6.69 and 6.61 per cent. GVA growth rates excluding government, agriculture and utilities were 8.76, 7.35, 6.47 and 5.73 per cent.

I cling to the hope that the BJP government will pause, take stock, pull back and steer the country on the path of good governance and development for all the people. We hope that jobs will be created, that investments will be made, that farmers will have better returns, that incomes will rise, that welfare measures for the poor will continue to be implemented, and that we will remain an open, free, liberal and democratic country.

WIN SOME, STEAL SOME

19 March 2017

The five state elections (Uttar Pradesh, Uttarakhand, Punjab, Goa and Manipur) had a common feature: it was a vote against the incumbent government. The BJP lost Punjab but won Uttar Pradesh and Uttarakhand convincingly. The Congress lost Uttarakhand but won Punjab convincingly. The Samajwadi Party lost Uttar Pradesh. Goa and Manipur delivered indecisive verdicts.

The winners formed the government in the states they won convincingly. In Goa and Manipur, the loser stole the election. The unwritten rule on government formation in a hung legislature—supported by precedent—is quite clear. The party that secured the highest number of seats would be invited first to form the government. If there was a pre-poll alliance and that alliance had secured the highest number of seats, the alliance parties would be invited to form the government. By that rule or convention, the Congress should have been invited to form the government in Goa (17/40 seats) and in Manipur (28/60 seats).

Obliging the Loser

The BJP was brazen and unapologetic. The governors of the two states were happy to oblige the BJP which came second both in Goa (13/40) and in Manipur (21/60). That is why I say the elections in the two states were stolen. The precedents that deserved to be followed involved the Congress and the BJP. In the 1989 election, the Congress slipped badly, but it was the single largest party with 197 seats. The Janata Dal was a distant second with 143 seats. The President, R. Venkataraman, invited Rajiv Gandhi, the leader of the single largest party, to form the government. Rajiv Gandhi politely declined, taking the view that the verdict was against the Congress government. He set a fine example. Thereafter, the President invited V.P. Singh to form the government, and the rest is history. All three key players—R. Venkataraman, Rajiv Gandhi and V.P. Singh—played according to the rulebook. The president did not act in haste, the process took a few days, but no calamity fell on the nation during that period.

There was a sequel after about nine months. The Janata Party split, V.P. Singh resigned, and the president began the search for a new government. Once again, he invited Rajiv Gandhi. Once again, Rajiv Gandhi declined and suggested that Chandra Shekhar, the leader of the breakaway group of the Janata Dal, may be invited and the Congress would support him. Always the cautious player, R. Venkataraman took a letter from the Congress promising support to Chandra Shekhar and then invited the latter to form the government.

The next precedent was even more compelling. In the 1996 election, the BJP emerged as the single largest party (161 seats), but it was quite apparent that it could not cobble together a coalition or prove its majority in the Lok Sabha. The Congress (140 seats) offered outside support to a non-BJP government. Yet, Mr Atal Bihari Vajpayee, as the leader of the single largest party, got the invitation. His government lost a vote of confidence on the thirteenth day. Mr H.D. Deve Gowda got the next invitation.

Convention, Now Law

The only exception to the rule—or convention—that the leader of the single largest party should get the first invitation to form the government is in the case of a pre-poll alliance. A pre-poll alliance can be regarded as one political group or entity and, if it emerged as the single largest group, it would earn the right to form the government. The case of a post-poll alliance is different. A post-poll alliance can indeed be formed, but it will get the right to form the government only when the single largest party or a pre-poll alliance had failed in its attempt to form a government.

Besides, the principles set out above are no longer mere conventions or moral prescriptions. The principles are the law according to Mr Fali Nariman, an acknowledged expert on constitutional law. Five-, seven- and nine-judge benches of the Supreme Court have affirmed these principles. Reference may be made to the Rameshwar Prasad (2006) case and the Nabam Rebia (2016) case. Mr Nariman rued 'why the Supreme Court's order on Tuesday (14 March) completely missed this point'.

Mischief at Large

Goa was an egregious case. The incumbent BJP government had suffered a crushing defeat. Six of the eight ministers, including the chief minister, had lost their seats. The politically correct thing to do was to sit in the Opposition. Marshalling its seemingly limitless resources, in a matter of hours, the BJP inveigled small parties into its net, and staked claim the day after the results were officially declared. An obligated governor was too happy to recognize an opportunistic post-poll alliance that included the Goa Forward Party (GFP) that had run a robust anti-BJP campaign and fought the election as an undeclared ally of the Congress! The GFP got its reward—all three GFP MLAs were sworn in as ministers!

Manipur was a similar case. The Congress government had been defeated but the Congress was the single largest party. Therefore, the Congress should have been invited.

Of course, aberrations have occurred in the past, but that cannot be a reason to commit the mischief again. The BJP's victories in Uttar Pradesh and Uttarakhand were sufficient to seal its place as the dominant political party in India today. There was absolutely no need to bring Goa and Manipur into the BJP column.

By stealing the elections, the BJP has diminished India's reputation as a democracy.

THAT SINKING FEELING—1

7 May 2017

Once in a few years, there arrives a moment when the whole nation appears to share the same mood—of celebration or anger or despair. Such a moment may have arrived in India in 2017. You will find ample evidence of what I am saying in centre-page articles, columns, interviews, social media and even in some editorials. The narrative that seems to emerge from various strands of conversations and comments is that 'the Centre cannot hold' and the India that we had imagined in 2014 'is falling apart'. There is, of course, a determined push to sell a counter-narrative, as was done in September 2016 (surgical strike) and November 2016 (demonetisation), but the attempted counter-narrative seems rather weak against the facts.

Numbers Don't Lie

Let me begin with the indisputable facts. There is a rise in violence, be it terrorist incidents in J&K or attacks by Maoists in Naxal-affected areas. The numbers of the deaths tell the story:

	2014			2015			2016			2017 (up to April)*		
	C	T/M	SF	C	T/M	SF	C	T/M	SF	C	T/M	SF
J&K	28	110	47	17	108	39	15	150	82	9	43	15
Naxal-affected Areas	222	63	88	171	89	59	213	222	65	59	45	34

*tentative

C: Civilians; T/M: Terrorists/Militants; SF: Security forces

Maoists Regaining Ground?

The picture is dismal in Naxal-affected areas and the deterioration is visible. The epicentre is Chhattisgarh, where a BJP government under Mr Raman Singh has been in office for 14 years. Mr Raman Singh has perfected the art of hiding his government's total ineptitude, and deflecting criticism to the central government. It has also not helped that the NDA government has reversed major policy initiatives taken by the UPA government. The Backward Regions Grant Fund was scrapped. The Integrated Action Plan (IAP) that had placed funds in the hands of each collector to meet the felt needs of the people (and had won universal praise) was abruptly withdrawn. The MGNREGS was underfunded. The Scheduled Tribes and Other Traditional Forest Dwellers (Recognition of Forest Rights) Act, 2006, was diluted. The cumulative effect of these thoughtless actions was that the district administrations had nothing at their disposal to counter the charges of the Maoists of neglect and exploitation by a 'capitalist' system. Maoists thrive when there is support from the local population. The local people can be weaned away from the influence of Maoists only if the State is seen to be recognizing the rights of the people, especially the tribal people, and addressing their grievances and needs. Since the State seems to have withdrawn from actively engaging with the people—and the only arm of the State that is visible is the security forces—the Maoists seem to have regained their influence and the capacity to strike.

Losing or Lost the Valley

The most rapid deterioration in the security situation has occurred in the Kashmir Valley. It is clearly a throwback to 2010. Mr A.S. Dulat, a former director of the Research and Analysis Wing (R&AW), has said that the situation is worse than what it was in 1990 (when a BJP-supported government was in office). He is right, the numbers do not lie. The security forces are killing more terrorists but they are also losing more of their own, and neither the success nor the sacrifice is bringing normalcy to the Kashmir Valley. What has changed for the worse is the nature of the protest and the composition of the protesters. Never before have young girls indulged in stone-pelting, never before have mothers said that they cannot restrain their children, never before have there been such widespread protests without a visible leader, and never before have people wedged themselves between the security forces and suspected terrorists during a gunbattle. These are ominous portents. To peddle the counter-narrative, the drum-beating has started, aided and abetted by sections of the media that want a spectacular blow up either in the Kashmir Valley or in Pakistan. It is, once again, nationalism vs liberalism, unity vs *azaadi* (freedom), ostracism vs engagement, and bullets vs talks—none of which is relevant to restoring normalcy or finding a solution. Thanks to the binary rhetoric, both normalcy and solution have become more distant and unattainable.

Heed Independent Voices

I am a voice of the Opposition. I know such voices are brushed aside, but there are other voices. Listen to Mr M.K. Narayanan, a former national security advisor (NSA): 'Peace cannot be enforced by authoritarian means or by fiat' and 'What is most crucial is to make an open and impassioned appeal for peace in the Valley accompanied by meetings and consultations at several levels'. Listen to Mr A.S. Dulat: 'There is a sense of hopelessness. They aren't afraid to die. Villagers, students and even girls are coming out on the streets. This has never happened in the past' and 'Kashmiris are disappointed to see that nothing happened after (Mr) Modi took over. Where has (Mr) Vajpayee's *insaaniyat ka daira* (ambit of humanity) gone?'

Now, please read my columns on J&K that appeared between April and September 2016. That was the period when the government was losing control. Then, I wrote on 16 April 2017, when my private view was that the government had lost control. Two subjects—Maoism and Kashmir—have consumed the space for this column and seem enough to explain that sinking feeling. There is more.

THAT SINKING FEELING—2

14 May 2017

Everyone has likes and dislikes. They concern food, clothes, books, friends, neighbours, politics and practically everything else. That is why it is said 'one man's food is another man's poison.'

Family, culture and religion have a profound influence on one's likes and dislikes. One may argue for what one likes ('vegetarian food is sufficient for a strong body'), or one may argue against what one dislikes ('English must be replaced in the conduct of official business'), but one cannot kill or cause injury.

Violence Everywhere

India has become a killing field, not only because of militants and Maoists, but because of likes and dislikes. There is actual killing, taking a life, an act that the law describes as murder. Akhlaq, a poor farmer, was killed by a mob because the mob believed that he had kept the flesh of a cow—beef—at his home. Pehlu Khan, a dairy farmer, and his sons had bought two cows and were transporting them to their farm. They were stopped by a group of self-appointed *gau rakshaks* (protectors of the cow), beaten, and Pehlu Khan was killed. In both cases, the mob or the group did not like the idea that someone may be eating beef.

There is violence short of murder as well. A crowd led by an elected representative defied the law, took out a 'religious' procession, was stopped by the police, went on a rampage, vandalized the home of the superintendent of police and terrorized his wife and small children. In this case, the crowd and the elected representative did not like the fact that another religious group had a long custom of taking out a procession.

There is vigilantism. A young couple (not married) rode a rickshaw to a cinema. The police apprehended them, took them to a police station, questioned them for hours, and finally let them off with a severe 'warning'. The police personnel belonged to a group officially designated as 'anti-Romeo squad' and they were tasked to prevent young couples from using public streets or spaces. Non-police groups did the same thing in Kochi and elsewhere. An outfit called the Hindu Yuva Vahini became the enforcer of morals in Uttar Pradesh.

Whither Secularism?

There are communal clashes. There are caste clashes. Leaders jumped into the fray, not to condemn the clashes or to make peace, but to find 'reasons' why the clashes were justified.

There is fear. Places of worship are desecrated. Religious minorities live in fear. Dalits live in fear. A Dalit is damned if he does (skins a carcass) and damned if he doesn't (refuses to skin a carcass). Rohith Vemula wrote 'My birth is my fatal accident'. Girls live in fear of harassment if they are seen with boys or wear jeans or have a drink at a bar. Tribals live in fear that they will be deprived of their land and forest rights.

There is polarization. Without a shred of evidence to support the implied charge of discrimination, it was declared 'if land is given for a *kabristan*, equal land must be given for a *shamshan*' and 'if there is electricity for Eid, there must be equal amount of electricity for Diwali'.

Rise of Intolerance

There is intolerance of dissent. Mr Sitaram Yechury was disinvited to a scheduled lecture in Nagpur. My talk at IIT Delhi was cancelled a day before it was scheduled. Ms Priya Pillai was stopped from boarding a flight to London where she was due to address British Parliamentarians on human rights. Lest they become too vocal, non-government organizations are threatened with investigations or cancellation of registration under the Foreign Contribution (Regulation) Act or the Income-tax Act.

There is ideological profiling. RSS *swayamsevaks* (volunteers) were appointed as governors. Heads of educational and cultural institutions were selected from a small group of right-wing, conservative intellectuals. Textbooks in Haryana were screened by a committee headed by a self-confessed Hindutva ideologue.

There is insult. Some religions and their followers were ridiculed. Agents were paid to troll journalists and columnists. There is little or no counterargument, only abuse in the filthiest language.

There is the spectre of an Orwellian state. Aadhaar has transformed from voluntary to mandatory. It was conceived as an aid to DBT schemes; it has become a precondition to exercise legal rights such as travel or buying property or paying taxes. Citizens' data is collected by numerous agencies without a law on data security or data privacy. Data-leak is commonplace. The government brazenly told the Supreme Court that no person has an absolute right over his or her body!

In the ranking of 198 countries on religious intolerance, India stands at fourth from the bottom. In the World Press Freedom Index of 180 countries, India's rank has dropped from 131 to 140.

It would be foolish to attribute all of the above to the period after the NDA government assumed office in May 2014. These ills were indeed present before. A hierarchical society is inherently authoritarian and intolerant. The difference is this: then, when these ills manifested themselves, persons holding positions of high authority condemned them and the nation bowed its head in shame; now, there is scant condemnation and absolutely no shame.

Secularism is derided. Liberalism is challenged. Dissent is sedition. Questioning the government (or the Army Chief or the RBI Governor) is anti-national. The path to '*Sabka Saath, Sabka Vikas*' is paved with authoritarianism, uniformity and implicit obedience to the will of the rulers.

As that sinking feeling deepens, there is more.

THAT SINKING FEELING—3

21 May 2017

Speaking truth to power is a rare virtue. Dr Arvind Subramanian, the CEA, has that virtue. Like his predecessor, he has brought original thinking to the Economics Division; like his predecessor, he has found the freedom to speak on a variety of subjects; but unlike in the case of his predecessor, he is not always consulted (e.g., demonetisation).

I have great respect for Dr Subramanian as an economist. Recently, on two occasions he spoke the blunt truth. The first was the famous V.K.R.V. Rao Memorial Lecture when he bemoaned the fact that experts tend to 'find ex-post logic to attribute merit to government decisions'.

Sectors in Trouble

On 16 May 2017, he made important statements on the state of the economy. Among other things, he said, 'India's current employment challenge is particularly difficult as sectors that did well in generating jobs in the country's previous economic boom years—information technology (IT), construction and agriculture—are in trouble now.' Observing that many things need to be done to increase employment, Dr Subramanian said, 'First, we need to get the economy growing at 8 per cent to 10 per cent rate because we know that if you have dynamism, it can create opportunities for employment. That is absolutely crucial…you can't have employment growing if the economy is growing at 3–4 per cent.'

The boom years were 2004–09. In that five-year period, the average growth rate was 8.4 per cent. Following the international financial crisis, thanks to increased spending, the economy continued to grow at a robust rate. Naturally, jobs were created, although not as many as the country needed. Today, if jobs are not being created, it is because we are not growing at the rate that we are told to believe.

Agriculture is the principal source of livelihood for about 60 million owner-households and about 20 million landless labourer-households. The construction industry provides 35 million jobs. IT supports 3.7 million jobs in India and is a natural choice for the educated, upwardly mobile middle class. If these three sectors languish, new jobs will not be created. There is evidence that jobs have been lost. In IT alone, the estimated job loss in the near term is 200,000 to 600,000.

People's Perceptions

Achhe din is about security—national security, internal security, physical security of the individual, food security, job security and so on. I have written about national and internal security and about the threat to liberty. They may appear to be distant concerns for the overwhelming majority of the people (actually, they are not), but food security and job security are deeply felt concerns in every home.

If there is not enough food in a home, there can be no *achhe din*. If there are not enough jobs for the millions that enter the labour market every year, there can be no *achhe din*.

Upon completion of three years in office, questions will be asked. A newspaper considered very friendly to the government did ask some questions and the answers are revealing:

1. Have healthcare facilities and services in your city improved? 58 per cent said NO.
2. Do you feel crimes against women and children have reduced? 60 per cent said NO.

3. Do you feel prices of essential items and cost of living have reduced? 66 per cent said NO.
4. Do you feel the unemployment rate has reduced? 63 per cent said NO.
5. Has corruption reduced as a result of demonetisation? 47 per cent said NO and 37 per cent said YES.

The respondents were also asked, 'Which according to you has been the most effective mission of the government?' The only growth/job related scheme that was picked was 'Make in India', and this was chosen by a mere 8 per cent.

Economists will reach the same conclusions when they look at the economic indicators: declining GFCF, negative credit growth to industry, a large number of stalled projects, and acute distress in the farm sector (with farm wages growing at barely 4 per cent annually). The immediate impact is on jobs: new jobs not being created and many existing jobs in danger of being axed.

Tackle Joblessness

As the months roll by, despite the widespread support enjoyed by the prime minister, the clamour for jobs will get louder. Where are the jobs? There are no answers yet, except the flaunting of the magic number 7.5 per cent. Apparently, even the CEA does not believe that number. Otherwise, why would he point out that jobs are not being created and also say that 3–4 per cent growth will not create jobs? Is he hinting at something he knows but we don't know yet?

I am sure the CEA knows the answers lie in the following:

- Raise the investment to GDP ratio from 29.22 per cent (in 2016–17) to near the peak rate of 34–35 per cent achieved in 2007–08 and 2011–12.
- Reverse negative credit growth to micro, small and medium industries.
- Unblock stalled projects, particularly stalled infrastructure projects

whose number has increased from 766 in March 2014 to 893 in March 2016.
- Brush aside orthodoxy and give relief to farmers and raise the minimum wage for farm labour.

The elephant in the room is unemployment. Ask the youth (and their parents) about jobs. That sinking feeling will be complete.

'SHALL NOT LET ANYONE EAT'

9 July 2017

The late chief minister of Tamil Nadu, Jayalalithaa (or Amma), ruled with an iron hand. Under her, corruption flourished, but there was a functioning government too. Jayalalithaa has passed on (may her soul rest in peace) and it is no longer relevant to dwell upon that chapter in the history of Tamil Nadu. The important question now is, whither Tamil Nadu?

Jayalalithaa left behind a party and government that commanded the support of 135 members in a Legislative Assembly of 234 members, but she did not leave behind a designated successor. Perhaps she thought she would recover from her illness; perhaps she thought she had given enough indication that Mr O. Panneerselvam (her nominee on two earlier occasions) would be her successor; or perhaps she did not care what happened after her. However, two things were abundantly clear: (1) She did not give the slightest hint that Ms Sasikala would be her successor and (2) She did not readmit into the party Ms Sasikala's close relatives whom she had expelled in 2011.

The Coup and Consequences

Nevertheless, after Jayalalithaa passed on, Ms Sasikala staged a coup of sorts. She succeeded in first getting 'elected' as the general secretary of the party and then as leader of the legislature party. Just when she was poised to become chief minister, the judgement of the Supreme Court scuppered her ambitions. She hurriedly expelled Mr Panneerselvam and got the legislators to elect Mr E. Palaniswami as leader. The governor had no choice but to swear in Mr Palaniswami as chief minister.

Inevitably, the AIADMK split. To start with, there were two factions, but it is now apparent that there are three, if not four, factions. Despite the party's split, the government continues as if nothing had happened! The budget session is under way, but no one has called for a vote on any demand for grant or on any Bill, and no one has moved a motion of no-confidence! That is a modern-day miracle produced by the survival instincts of the legislators!

The popular belief is that the BJP is the puppeteer and is pulling the strings that hold the four factions. It could be part of the BJP's political strategy to carve out a space for itself in Tamil Nadu politics. It could be a tactical manoeuvre to garner the maximum number of votes for the election of the president and the vice-president. But if it is a long-term plan to win the AIADMK (or a major faction of the party) as an ally before forcing a mid-term poll in Tamil Nadu, then, serious questions will be raised.

Today, the AIADMK and the government are leaderless. Cases of corruption are exposed every day, but no one in the ruling faction of the AIADMK seems to care, smug in the belief that all factions of the party are in the clutches of the BJP-RSS, and nothing will be allowed that may lead to the defeat of the government.

Corruption Cases

After Jayalalithaa's demise, the following *major* cases of corruption have been unearthed in Tamil Nadu:

- Income tax searches on a mining group that started on 8 December 2016, led to the seizure of ₹135 crore and 177 kg of gold. The trail led to the office and residence of the chief secretary, who was replaced.

- On 4 April 2017, income tax officials searched the residence of the minister of health and claimed to have recovered documents, including a statement of money given to the chief minister and six ministers for distribution to voters in the by-election in the R.K. Nagar constituency.
- The by-election in R.K. Nagar constituency was cancelled because the Election Commission (EC) found evidence of large-scale distribution of money to voters. On 18 April 2017, the EC directed registration of cases against the chief minister and six ministers and their candidate.
- Two weeks ago, an investigative report in a newspaper revealed that a search had been conducted on 8 July 2016 on the premises of a gutka manufacturer and evidence of payments to a minister and senior police officials had been reportedly found. A report had been sent to the government soon afterwards but no action was taken.

Administrative corruption is rampant. There is a rate card in Tamil Nadu—a kind of menu of services and prices! A service can be obtained at the listed price. Under the current government, the system has been decentralized. Each MLA of the ruling faction is the virtual chief (minister) of his/her constituency; each minister is the virtual chief (minister) of his/her district.

What's BJP's Game?

Meanwhile, the finances of the state government are spinning out of control. The total debt at the end of 2017–18 will be ₹314,366 crore, which will be twice as much as the revenue projected at ₹159,363 crore. The state took over the loan of ₹22,815 crore of the power generation and distribution company (TANGEDCO) that caused the fiscal deficit to soar to a high of 4.58 per cent in 2016–17. The Debt to Gross State Domestic Product ratio has risen to 20.9 per cent. Capital expenditure, as a proportion of total expenditure, has declined in health and family welfare and in water supply, sanitation and urban development.

The government leaders in Tamil Nadu are 'eating' every day at every opportunity. The misgovernance is eating into the vitals of the state's economy. The prime minister said that he would not allow anyone to 'eat': his words were '*na khane doonga*'. Pray, then, will the BJP explain why it is breaking bread with such a party and government?

A COUNTER-NARRATIVE WILL EMERGE

6 August 2017

I am counting the number of people who have thrown in the towel. On Wednesday, 26 July 2017, it was Mr Nitish Kumar who abandoned his sword and steed and coronated himself (for the sixth time!) as the chief minister of Bihar. Given Bihar's poverty, joblessness and divisiveness, it is astonishing to know that there is someone who regards the chair of chief minister of that state as a prize to be won at the cost of his credibility and self-respect.

It is noisily propagated that the Modi–Shah juggernaut is unstoppable. One must board it quickly or make way respectfully or be run over mercilessly.

Since 26 July 2017, six Congress MLAs in Gujarat have signed the terms (visible and invisible) of surrender.

Vast sections of the media have been co-opted by the ruling party and the government. There are censors in newsrooms and editorial boards. Academia has been invaded; an invitation has been extended by the Vice-Chancellor of Jawaharlal Nehru University (JNU) to station an army tank on the campus. A retired major general hails the 'conquest' of JNU and promises to 'conquer Hyderabad and Jadavpur very soon'.

The Post-truth World

In the post-truth world, more and more people are believing what is not necessarily true.

They believe that ideology is dead. The only 'thing' you have to believe in is 'What's in it for me?' There is a lot in store for you if you believe in the muscular hyper-nationalism of the true (and only) nationalist Indians. The capture of institutions has just begun, there are many more, and they will throw up numerous opportunities for the true nationalists.

They believe that secularism is dead. State and religion will no longer be separate. The reinauguration of the Sardar Sarovar project after the height of the dam was raised to 138.72 metres will be sanctified by the presence and prayers of 2,000 priests from all over the country.

They believe that liberalism is dead. Mr Dina Nath Batra and Mr Pahlaj Nihalani, and others like them, will be the new commissars of right thought, right behaviour and right culture. Anything that does not have their approval shall be presumed to be wrong and, therefore, proscribed.

Liberty, Equality, Fraternity

They believe that liberty is dead. The only liberty that deserves to be recognized is defined in the following words: 'The only liberty worth having (is) the liberty of the State and of the individual within the State'. It is a minor detail that the definition was propounded by a gentleman named Mussolini.

They believe that equality is dead. There was never real equality in India—between religions, between castes, between genders. After the Vedic age, the laws of Manu were invented, varna was the prevailing dharma and India flourished without equality, so equality is no big deal. Those who had no part in making the Constitution of India have never accepted that equality was a legitimate national objective. It is, therefore, legitimate to ask for unequal rights and unequal privileges, especially if you belong to the Akhil Bharatiya Vidyarthi Parishad (ABVP, the students' wing of the BJP) or a *gau rakshak* group or the Vivekananda International Foundation, New Delhi.

They believe that fraternity is dead. It is perfectly normal to deny a house for rent to a Muslim or a Christian or a single woman or a non-vegetarian. It is perfectly legitimate to distinguish between non-Bengali maids and Bengali maids. It is perfectly legal to raze the hutments of the Bengali maids because they are anyway from Bangladesh.

They believe that English will be soon dead. The Committee of Parliament on Official Language will be requested to report regularly and frequently on ways and means to replace the use of English by the use of Hindi.

A Contrary View

I take a contrary view. I refuse to believe that liberty, equality or fraternity is or will be dead. These values are the soul of democracy and I believe that the people of India will never allow these values to die. Nor do I believe that the Indian people will abandon secularism and embrace Hindutva. The people know that secularism is the opposite of Hindutva. They also know that Hindutva will eventually mean a return to the days of domination of the upper castes and the oppression of the other backward castes and Dalits.

I refuse to believe that we live in a post-ideological world. Ideology is no longer captured by a single word like capitalism or communism. Every party has to craft its narrative taking into account changes in society and in the people's aspirations. Is not Hindutva an ideology? Does not the BJP audaciously pitch the philosophy of Savarkar, Golwalkar and Deendayal Upadhyaya as a counter-narrative to the philosophy of Mahatma Gandhi, Jawaharlal Nehru and Babasaheb Ambedkar?

I refuse to believe that the idea of India as enshrined in the Constitution can be destroyed. I refuse to believe that there are no Liu Xiaobos in India. I refuse to believe that the conscience of the media or authors or academia can be snuffed out forever. I am reassured by the statements of 87 academics (13 July 2017) and 114 defence veterans (1 August 2017).

It is true that, at present, the Opposition parties seem to have faltered in constructing an alternative narrative to majoritarianism and Hindutva. They have only themselves to blame, but I am absolutely certain that the suffering and struggles of different sections of the people will throw up a counter-narrative.

GOODS AND SERVICES TAX

After demonetisation, a flawed Goods and Services Tax was hastily implemented without adequate preparation. It turned out to be the disruptive event that it need not have been. I wrote sardonically that 'government did bad things in a big way or big things in a bad way'! In 2006, I had announced the intention to introduce GST and I was passionate about it during my term as finance minister. Hence I felt let down when it was implemented in a clumsy manner. I did my best to push the government to take corrective measures. Mercifully, some mistakes were corrected.

A TRYST WITH DESTINATION TAX *(With Reverent Homage and Apologies to Jawaharlal Nehru)*

25 June 2017

Not many years ago we made a tryst with destination tax, and now the time comes when we shall redeem our pledge, not wholly or in full measure, but we hope substantially.

At the stroke of the midnight hour, when businesspersons and consumers spend a sleepless night, India will awake to a new tax regime. A moment comes, which comes but rarely in our economic history, when we step out from the old to the new, when a century ends, and when the taxpayers of a nation, long oppressed, hope to find a new dawn.

It is fitting that at this solemn moment we take the pledge of dedication to the service of India and her taxpayers and to the still larger cause of tax justice.

At the dawn of this century—2005 to be exact—India started on her quest of GST and the intervening years are filled with disappointments and dashed hopes. Through good and ill fortune alike, she never lost sight of that quest or forgot the goal which gave her ambition. We end today a period of self-inflicted ill fortune and India unveils a new though imperfect tax regime.

The achievement we celebrate today is but a step, an opening of opportunity, to the greater triumphs and achievements that we hope for. Are we humble enough and wise enough to grasp this opportunity and accept the challenge of the future?

Endured the Pains

A new tax regime brings responsibility. The responsibility rests upon Parliament and the legislatures, sovereign bodies representing the sovereign people of India. Before the advent of GST, we had endured all the pains of blind opposition and our hearts are heavy with the memory of the lost years. Some of those pains continue even now. Nevertheless, we have put the past behind us and it is the future that beckons to us now.

The course of GST is not one of ease or resting but of incessant striving so that we may fulfil the pledges made in Parliament and the one that we shall take today. The service of taxpayers means the service of the millions who suffer multiplicity of taxes. It means levying a single, reasonable tax and collecting it fairly, avoiding harassment.

And so we have to labour and to work, and work hard, to give reality to the idea of GST.

Death has been said to be a certainty; so is taxation; and so also is tax harassment in this world that can no longer be tolerated as fair or just.

To the people of India, whose representatives we are, we make an appeal to join us with trust and hope in this great adventure. This is no time for hubris or haughtiness, no time for excuses or blaming others. We have to build a fair system of taxation where all producers and service providers may carry on their businesses.

A Fateful Moment

The appointed day has come—perhaps sooner than when we will be fully ready—and India stands forth again, after many stumbles and struggle, wary, uncertain, dissatisfied but hopeful. The past clings on to us still in some measure and we have to do much before we bring a true GST as well as petroleum and electricity and alcohol under GST. The turning point is in the near future, and our destiny will be written by us, a destiny that we will achieve or not, and others will write about.

It is a fateful moment for us in government, for all of India and for the states. A new tax regime rises, a promise made in 2006 has to be redeemed, a vision long cherished has to materialize. May the new regime never become oppressive and that hope never be betrayed!

We rejoice in that hope, even though clouds of unpreparedness surround us, and many people have forewarned us about the diarchy and difficult questions encompass us.

But a new regime brings responsibilities and burdens and we have to face them with a spirit of humility and willingness to correct errors.

We have often been unworthy opponents and have strayed from reason, but not only we but succeeding generations will remember the cause and bear the responsibility in their hearts. We should never allow that cause to be blown out, however tempting it may be to collect revenue by means fair or foul.

Our next thoughts must be of the original proponents and the scholars, who, without praise or reward, have espoused the cause of GST even unto ridicule.

The future beckons to us. Whither do we go and what shall be our endeavour? To bring a true GST and create a common market to the producers and consumers of India; to fight and end tax discrimination and harassment and oppression; to build up a competitive and dynamic economy; and to create determinative and adjudicatory institutions which will ensure justice and fairness to every producer and consumer.

One Nation, One Tax

We have hard work ahead. There is no resting for any one of us till we redeem our pledge in full, till we make the GST regime a truly One Nation, One Tax regime that it was intended to be.

We are inheritors of a sound economy, on the verge of higher growth, and we have to live up to the high standard of a few years ago. All of us, whatever position we hold, are equally responsible with equal rights and obligations. We cannot encourage high tax rates or high-handed tax administration, for no nation can have a vibrant economy whose tax laws and tax administration are narrow in thought or application.

To the states and the people of India, we send greetings and pledge ourselves to cooperate with them in furthering a fair and just tax regime.

And to the Indian taxpayer, the large, medium, small and micro businesses, and the individual households, we convey our eternal gratitude and we bind ourselves afresh to their service.

GET SET FOR TURBULENCE

2 July 2017

Nothing is more exhilarating than the promise of change, especially if it will be a change for the better. When it was first announced, the GST held that promise. It could still be a harbinger of a change for the better but, on a consideration of all the aspects, it seems to me the GST that came into effect on 1 July 2017 is an imperfect tax that will usher in a long period of turbulence.

As an idea, GST is unexceptionable. The Constitution of India (Art 301) promised a common market for India. However, the tax systems of our governments ensured that the country remained divided and fragmented. Inter-state barriers were erected, taxes were collected and evaded, rent-seeking flourished, and trade and commerce suffered.

VAT and GST are Major Reforms

The Value Added Tax (VAT) was the first comprehensive measure to bring uniformity in the tax systems of the states, but it was a state-level reform. Central tax laws (excise and service tax) and the principal state tax law (VAT) remained apart. Together, they imposed a heavy tax burden upon businesses, apart from the huge cost of complying with multiple taxes.

Once VAT was implemented throughout the country, the next logical step was GST. I seized the opportunity in 2006 to announce that it was our goal to implement GST by 2010. Delayed by seven years (does the finance minister remember who delayed it?), GST came into effect on 1 July 2017. I welcome GST but I wish that its launch was not surrounded by so many infirmities and uncertainties.

The positive aspects of GST need to be emphasized: One tax will subsume many taxes. It will capture nearly all commercial transactions above a certain threshold. It will eliminate cascading of the taxes levied at different stages of the value chain. It will enlarge the tax bases. Once these virtues had been acknowledged by all states, every effort should have been made to forge agreement on the crucial aspects of GST. In the absence of such an agreement, and because of a forced compromise, we are starting with a very imperfect GST.

The Design Flaws

- GST should have been one standard tax rate (with a concessional rate and a demerit rate), but it is not. We have rates of 0, .25, 3, 5, 12, 18, 28 and many higher rates depending upon the cesses that may be imposed on so-called sin goods.
- GST should have been under one unified tax authority, but it is not. There will be a diarchy. States and the Centre will divide the tax bases into 90:10 (for turnover under ₹15 million) and 50:50 (for turnover over ₹15 million). I suppose a lottery will decide whether one's tax authority will be the state government or the central government!
- GST should have stipulated fewer returns, but it does not. By the most charitable count, a business must file three returns a month and an annual return (total 37). If the business is a multi-state business, and the tax authority is the state government, that number must be multiplied by the number of states in which the business is located.
- GST should have eliminated classification disputes, but it does not. Fitment rates were changed many times. We saw interest group advocacy in full play. There will be disputes. Mr Veerappa Moily asked, 'Is KitKat chocolate or biscuit?', because chocolates and biscuits suffer different rates. I suppose the Supreme Court will be requested

to answer such questions in due course!

- GST should have reduced the discretion of the tax administrator, but it does not. On the contrary, draconian powers have been conferred on the 'Anti-profiteering Authority'. Whoever conceived of the bizarre idea had no knowledge of economics or business or markets or competition. A century of experience on economic regulation has passed him/her by. He/she is a holdover from a *dirigiste* regime that believed that the government knows best and it is the government's right and duty to tell business what it should sell and at what price.

Trial Run Would Have Helped

GST should have been given a trial run of two months before it was finally rolled out, but it was not. Every tax official who will administer GST at the state or central level should have been directed to spend two weeks working in the office of a small or medium business and actually 'filing' mock returns and 'paying' the calculated tax. During the trial period, the GST Network (GSTN) should have been tested in actual conditions and the glitches, if any, removed. The trial run would have boosted the confidence of businesses that they would be able to cope with the new regime. Of course that would have meant a short deferment of the final rollout of the GST, but a stubborn government refused to pay heed to well-intentioned advice from many quarters.

The worst tendencies of the Indian State and politics and business have found their way into the design of the GST that was launched on 1 July 2017. Many of the flaws in the design were the result of forced political compromise. It seems to me too much has been compromised and for reasons that are not apparent.

Anyway, we have a baby. It is not a bonny baby, it has some birth defects, it must be carefully nurtured, but it is our baby and let me therefore welcome the new baby.

AGAINST CONSUMER AND GOOD ECONOMICS

24 September 2017

I remember the day in July 2008 when the price of crude oil touched $147 a barrel.

I remember the day when the King of Saudi Arabia convened a conference of oil-producing and oil-consuming countries to discuss the crisis of rising oil prices. I led the Indian delegation that included Murli Deora, then minister of petroleum. At the conference, we proposed a price band: an upper limit which will not be crossed by the oil-producing countries and a lower limit which will not be breached by the oil-consuming countries. It was sort of mutual guarantees by both sides. Everyone nodded in sage agreement, but there was no agreement.

Throughout the period of the UPA government (2004–14), except for a brief interlude, crude oil prices ruled high. Taxing petroleum products, especially petrol and diesel, was unavoidable because we needed the revenue and we needed to curb consumption. Subsidizing some petroleum products, especially kerosene and LPG, was also unavoidable because we needed to soften the impact on the poor and we needed to save the forests. It was a balancing act that was performed under great stress. Nevertheless, whenever there was a price increase, the UPA government was savaged by the Opposition, notably by the BJP.

Commodities and Oil Prices Collapse

Since 2014, the oil world has turned upside down. Demand for commodities, including oil, has collapsed. New and cheaper methods have been found to produce shale oil. The price of crude oil has declined sharply. Russia witnessed a recession. Saudi Arabia was obliged to impose an income tax on a section of its citizens. Venezuela is bankrupt. Oil consumers got a windfall.

India is the exception. India got a windfall, but the Indian consumer pays the same price! See Table below:

	May 2014	Sept 2017
Average Price of Brent Crude Oil (USD per barrel)	109.68	55.68
Exchange Rate	59.31	63.99
Average Price of Crude Oil Per Litre (INR)	40.90	22.40
Price (Delhi) of Petrol Per Litre	71.41	70.52
Price (Delhi) of Diesel Per Litre	56.71	58.79
Tax Component (Centre & State) of Petrol Prices	21.41	36.47
Tax Component (Centre & State) of Diesel Prices	9.97	26.01

If we assume that the quantity of petrol and diesel consumed in the country has remained the same, the governments are garnering by way of tax revenue twice the amount they collected in May 2014. The main culprit is the central government: on every litre of petrol it is collecting ₹21.48 as against ₹9.48 in May 2014, and on every litre of diesel it is collecting ₹17.33 as against ₹3.56 in May 2014. Actually, consumption has increased by 17 per cent in the last three years, so the gross collection at higher tax rates is even more!

Easy Money

The tax collected is easy money. Easy money becomes an addiction. Excise duties on petrol and diesel have been raised on 11 occasions by the NDA government since May 2014. On these two products alone, the central government earned ₹327,550 crore in 2016–17 (RE).

Average Brent crude oil price has declined by 49 per cent since May 2014. Factoring that decline, and if the central tax component had remained at the level of May 2014, the retail price of petrol should have come down by 19 per cent and diesel by 21 per cent. They haven't and are actually at the same or higher level.

We are in this situation because we have a greedy government that believes in 'tax and spend'. It has to find the money for 'government expenditure' since that is the only engine of growth that is running (read 'Clueless in New Delhi', *The Indian Express,* 17 September 2017). The current government believes that middle-class and lower middle-class consumers who own vehicles should pay the hefty taxes because, according to the new minister of tourism, 'they are not starving'!

If prices of petroleum products are reduced, reflecting economic realities, the government will benefit in many ways: the subsidy expenditure on kerosene and LPG will be lower and the railway, defence and other departments will incur lower fuel costs.

Anti-consumer

Because of the predatory taxation policy of the government, the decline in the average price of crude oil has had no impact on inflation. Transport costs remain high. Consumers' capacity to spend on other goods and services is constrained. Private consumption has increased barely at 6.66 per cent in Q1 of 2017–18. Besides, the competitiveness of Indian producers and service providers has been eroded vis-à-vis their foreign competitors. It is also unwise to rely on heavy taxation of one commodity; if the price of crude oil rises sharply, the government would have to forgo revenue or inflict a huge burden on the people. Viewed from any angle, maintaining retail prices of petrol and diesel at the same level they were in May 2014 is anti-consumer, anti-competition and anti-economic principles.

Resentment is building up among the people. There have been protests in many parts of the country. The government is deaf to the pleas to lower the taxes and pass the benefit of lower crude oil prices to the consumers.

In the context of demonetisation, Dr Manmohan Singh said it was 'organised loot and legalized plunder'. In my view, those words aptly describe the NDA government's policy of taxation of petrol and diesel.

GST UNRAVELS, QUICK FIXES NOT ANSWER

5 November 2017

The idea of a GST was, and is, a good idea. It is a tax that is in force in about 160 countries with some variations in each country, but the basic principle is that it is a one-rate tax applicable to all goods and services, unless they are exempted.

The CEA, in his report on the revenue neutral rate (RNR), recommended a rate of 15 or 15.5 per cent. Taking note of the difficult transition path from VAT to GST and from Service Tax to GST, he also acknowledged the need to have a merit rate (RNR minus) and a demerit rate (RNR plus). That would have preserved the essential principle of a GST while enabling a smooth transition.

Not True GST

The NDA/BJP government violated the principles of a true GST, brushed aside the report of the CEA and constructed its own GST. Given the BJP's penchant for inventing acronyms, it could have given the tax a name other than GST, because what we have got is not a true GST nor a 'good and simple tax'. Mr Rahul Gandhi trashed the tax as Gabbar Singh Tax, and that label has stuck to the tax. It will take a lot of undoing and repair to shake off that label.

The GST and its implementation were flawed in concept, design, rate or rates, inclusion and exclusion criteria, exemption thresholds, advocacy and dissemination, compliance requirements, infrastructure, preparedness, training and so on. Nothing about the GST introduced on 1 July 2017 was right.

The consequences of a deeply flawed GST and hasty implementation are there for all to see. The biggest sufferers are MSMEs, especially manufacturing businesses. Micro enterprises (a source of self-employment) have closed down and gone out of business. Small enterprises (usually with family members as workers) are struggling to survive and many have closed shop with little hope of resuming their business. Medium enterprises (the source of employment for 90 per cent of the non-agricultural workforce) are barely able to keep their heads above the water but have paid a heavy price: cutting back on production, reducing the workforce, borrowing for additional working capital, paying large amounts for professional help in complying with the law, and living in constant fear of the tax officials.

The government haughtily rejected the criticism made in Parliament when the law was being debated. It brushed aside the well-intentioned advice of business associations and tax practitioners. It entrusted the drafting and implementation of the laws to civil servants who had never run a business in their lives nor risked a rupee of their own money in starting or supporting a business. The result was the innumerable flaws and the enormous hardship heaped on the business community and the consumers.

Mr Fixit at Work

It is only when the 'tax problem' threatened to become a 'political problem' that the government seems to have woken up from its slumber.

Now, the government is struggling to 'fix' the problems in the GST regime. The desperation is visible: look at the number of changes made and the deferments and waivers granted in the four months since the GST was implemented with effect from 1 July 2017. And they are not done yet; there will be another meeting of the GST Council on 11 November 2017 to 'fix' more problems and, believe me, that will not be the last meeting called for the purpose!

I counted 27 reductions of rates; 7 prescriptions of rates; 22 exemptions; one waiver; and 15 extensions of time. The 11th Amendment to the GST Rules was made on 28 October 2017. Many of the changes were to correct obvious errors in the design and structure, especially the provisions concerning MSMEs. Some were to defer controversial or complicated provisions such as the reverse charge mechanism, application of TDS/TCS and the e-way bill system. Common sense seems to have returned after subjecting MSMEs to four months of hardship.

Need Complete Overhaul

Some things, however, cannot be 'fixed' quickly—for example, the multiple rate structure, the HSN classification, the exclusion of electricity and petroleum products, the cascading effect, the 'pay first, refund later' rule and the diarchic control. Changes in these elements will require a complete overhaul of the present GST structure and extensive amendments to the laws. That seems beyond the comprehension of the government.

Criticism of the government was not confined to India. *The Financial Times* reported stories of small businesses that had shut down. It quoted Dr Jahangir Aziz, a Singapore-based economist, who said that the government had underestimated the impact of transition, both in terms of the hit to growth and how long the dampening effect could last. *The Economist*, in a scathing editorial, recalled the hardship and disruption caused by demonetisation and said, 'The shambolic implementation of the GST is likely to make matters worse.' The conclusion was devastating: 'The BJP is not that interested in policy. It offers voters mainly distraction.'

That the economy has taken two damaging hits is a fact. That the growth rate of GDP has declined in six quarters from 9.1 per cent to 5.7 per cent is a fact. It is possible that 5.7 per cent is the bottom of the decline and the growth curve may turn upward. That can give bragging rights to the government, but the undeniable facts are that businesses have closed down and jobs have been lost.

There is no Quick Fix for that.

FOREIGN POLICY

There is only one column in this section. It was on the standoff between China and India in the Dolam plateau that lies within the Doklam region. The afterword on the subject from the government was that the crisis had been resolved, and it was implied that India had scored a point over China. However, China seemed to have another view as was evident from the contradictory statements made by the two countries following the meeting of the two foreign ministers in December 2017. I fear that we have not heard the last word on the subject.

PING PONG OF WORDS, OR WORSE?

30 July 2017

The world is nowhere close to embracing Pope John's impassioned declaration 'No more war, never again war'.

Since the end of World War II, the world has witnessed hot wars, cold wars, civil wars, secessionist wars, jihadi wars, invasion, annexation and many other kinds of violent conflict. Not a day has passed without loss of lives in armed conflicts.

India and China fought a war in 1962. After the War ended, there was a fragile peace. In 1988, Rajiv Gandhi was invited to China. It was a historic visit. Remember the famous l-o-n-g handshake with Deng Xiaoping? The two countries agreed to talk to each other and resolve all differences about the border/boundary through negotiations. Shortly afterwards, special representatives were appointed.

India, China Gained Time

From time to time, there were incidents. Talks followed. Issues were resolved. More recently, armed conflict was avoided in Depsang (2013) and Demchok and Chumar (2014). 'Understandings' were arrived at. In 2012, an agreement was reached that the tri-junction issue between India and China will be resolved in consultation with the third party, Bhutan, in whose territory the tri-junction was located (and because of the special relationship of India with Bhutan).

Both countries, by avoiding armed conflict, gained valuable time to focus on economic development. China is well on its way to be described as a middle-income country; it has lifted all but 5 per cent of its vast population of 1,380 million from poverty. It has become the world's factory and its exports have helped it build a foreign exchange reserve of over $3,000 billion. It is a nuclear power, it has the largest active standing army in the world, it has the capacity to venture deep into the South China Sea and the Indian Ocean, and it is believed to have the capacity to strike at distant targets.

India has also made considerable progress notwithstanding loud noises that nothing had happened in the years up to 2014 (including, presumably, the Vajpayee years 1998–2004), but India is a few steps behind China. Since 1991, India has lifted over 250 million people out of poverty. Its foreign exchange reserves stand at $380 billion. It is a nuclear power, it has the second largest active standing army in the world, and it has the capacity to defend itself against any aggression by a foreign power.

For these very reasons, India and China should guard against being drawn into a shooting war. Every time—and I mean, every time—diplomacy must succeed and the sabres must remain sheathed. Wordfare (if I may coin a word) should not become warfare.

Is it Different Now?

The development near the tri-junction of India-Bhutan-China in the Dolam plateau (that lies in the Doklam region) on 16 June 2017, should remain an 'incident' that can be resolved through talks. But, I am afraid, indications are to the contrary. The 'incident' has acquired sinister proportions. No one can deny that there is a marked difference between the 2017 incident and the incidents of 2013 and 2014.

Just look at the public statements of India and China. On the Indian side, statements have been made by the Army Chief (8 June 2017), Ministry of External Affairs (30 June), the finance minister (30 June), the foreign secretary (11 July), the minister of state in the PMO (12 July), and external affairs minister (20 July). The responders on the side of China have been only 'spokespersons' of the Foreign Ministry or the Army—until Mr Wang Yi, the foreign minister, spoke on 25 July 2017, at Bangkok. Besides, the true intent of China was reflected in stinging write-ups that appeared in *Global Times* and *Xinhua*. The language of the Chinese side's responses was, to put it mildly, undiplomatic.

What has changed? If there is a change in China's attitude to India, what are the circumstances that led to the change? I believe the Government of India when it articulated its position in the following words: 'India is deeply concerned at the recent Chinese actions and has conveyed to the Chinese government that such construction would represent a significant change of status quo with serious security implications for India.' However, that is not enough. The government owes a duty to the people of India to explain what has changed and why it has changed. Such a statement can come only from the prime minister.

Will it Stop with Words?

The rhetoric on the Chinese side is getting shriller by the day. Every overture by India has been spurned. The NSA's visit to China was first belittled, then a perfunctory reference was made to talks between the NSAs during which China set forth its position on 'bilateral issues and major problems'. Contrary to the usual rules of diplomacy, China seems to have left no negotiating room for itself. It has laid down a non-negotiable condition and, at the same time, closed every avenue for negotiation. *Xinhua* wrote on 15 July 2017, 'China has made it clear that there is no room for negotiations on this incident and India must withdraw its border-crossing troops from Doklam.'

Discerning observers in India are naturally concerned but there is no such concern expressed by anyone in China. The United States was the first country to openly advise restraint and urge talks. Many other countries which had been briefed by both India and China have strangely remained silent.

The gathering clouds are ominous. I am clear in my mind that under no circumstances should there be a shooting war between India and China. I am sure that is also the view of the Government of India, but I doubt if it is the view of the Government of China. Only time will tell what and when misjudgements were made.

LAW

The Supreme Court of India delivered a historic judgement in the case of *Justice K.S. Puttaswamy.* The Court ruled unanimously that privacy was a fundamental right. The argument of the central government, supported by several BJP-ruled state governments, was comprehensively rejected. The funny aspect of the case was, after the verdict, the government claimed victory! I think one battle has been won, but many more remain. The other column in this section is on the Finance Bill and how the device of a Money Bill was being misused.

THE INTOXICATION OF ABSOLUTE POWER

2 April 2017

The Finance Bill is, usually, the most important Bill on the annual legislative agenda of the finance minister. Policy decisions are first taken by the Department of Revenue with the approval of the finance minister and these decisions are conveyed to the draftsmen. Dozens of officers, including officers of the Ministry of Law, spend more than a hundred hours to draft the Finance Bill. Senior officers spend many hours poring over the draft to satisfy themselves that the policy decisions taken earlier have been accurately reflected in the Bill.

The buck for the policy decisions stops at the table of the finance minister. The buck for the drafting should also stop at the table of the finance minister, especially if he is also a person trained in law.

I have three issues concerning Finance Bill, 2017.

An Assault on the Constitution

A Finance Bill is, pre-eminently, a Money Bill under Article 110 of the Constitution of India (see box below), but is Finance Bill, 2017, a Money Bill? I do not believe that Mr Arun Jaitley does not know the scope of and the limitations imposed by Article 110. Nor do I believe that Mr Jaitley thinks that the word '*only*' is otiose. Nor do I believe that he is unaware of the passages quoted by Mr Kapil Sibal in the course of the debate in the Rajya Sabha:

Erskine May had said: 'A bill which contains any of the enumerated matters and nothing besides is indisputably a Money Bill. If it contains any other matters, then, unless these are subordinate matters incidental to any of the matters so contained in the Bill, it is not a Money Bill.'

G.V. Mavalankar, the first Speaker, had ruled in 1956: 'I would normally urge upon the Finance Minister, not only he, but also his successors to see that only those provisions which relate to the raising of taxations should be included in the Bill. The procedure should be followed, and no other provision should be given attention to unless it is absolutely consequential.'

Article 110

For the purposes of this Chapter, a Bill shall be deemed to be a Money Bill if it contains only provisions dealing with all or any of the following matters, namely:

a) the imposition, abolition, remission, alteration or regulation of any tax;
b) the regulation of the borrowing of money or the giving of any guarantee by the Government of India, or the amendment of the law with respect to any financial obligations undertaken or to be undertaken by the Government of India;
c) the custody of the Consolidated Fund or the Contingency Fund of India, the payment of moneys into or the withdrawal of moneys from any such Fund;
d) the appropriation of moneys out of the Consolidated Fund of India;
e) the declaring of any expenditure to be expenditure charged on the Consolidated Fund of India or the increasing of the amount of any such expenditure;
f) the receipt of money on account of the Consolidated Fund of India or the public account of India or the custody or issue of such money or the audit of the accounts of the Union or of a State; or
g) any matter incidental to any of the matters specified in sub clause (a) to (f)

Finance Bill, 2017, is an assault on Article 110 of the Constitution. Fifty-five of the 189 clauses of the Finance Bill have nothing to do with taxation—Clause (a)—or have any connection with any of the Clauses (b) to (g) of sub-Article (1) of Article 110. Further, these 55 clauses are not consequential or incidental to the other clauses of the Finance Bill that are concerned with taxation. These suspect clauses have been smuggled into the Finance Bill by the finance minister against his legal conscience. The real purpose was to avoid scrutiny of the Bill by the Rajya Sabha. His comeuppance will be when the Supreme Court rules on what shall and what shall not be included in a Money Bill.

Tax Terrorism

The assessee had one shield against arbitrary actions by tax officials: it was the requirement that the tax officer shall have 'reason to believe' and shall record the reasons. The reasons must be disclosed to the assessee; the assessee may challenge the so-called reasons in a court of law, and if the court held that the reasons were non-existent, irrelevant or unjustified the court would quash the proceedings. Finance Bill, 2017, has changed the law. Clauses 50 and 51 have introduced an *Explanation* to Sections 132 and 132A of the Income-tax Act that reads: 'For the removal of doubts, it is hereby declared that the reason to believe, as recorded by the income-tax authority under this sub-section, shall not be disclosed to any person or any authority or the Appellate Tribunal.'

The *Explanation* is against settled law. The law is being 'unsettled' with retrospective effect from 1 April 1962 or 1 October 1975! If the assessee is not given the reasons, how will the assessee challenge the so-called reasons and ask the court to quash the proceedings? Why should the assessee go through proceedings up to the stage of the Income-tax Appellate Tribunal without having an effective opportunity to challenge the initiation of the proceedings? Clauses 50 and 51 are suspect and the battle will now move to the courts.

Political Funding

I support the efforts to cleanse political funding. I welcome the idea of electoral bonds. Under the provisions of Finance Bill, 2017, a donor may purchase bonds and only the issuing bank(s) will know the name of the donor/purchaser. The donor can donate the bonds to one or more political parties but neither the donor nor the donee-political party is required to disclose the names in their returns! If the objective is transparency and clean political funding, why should the names of donors and donee-political parties be kept secret? Finance Bill, 2017, will promote money laundering. Corporates and other donors should be warned: nothing will prevent a future government from amending the law and making public the names of all donors and donee-political parties.

Parliament is only one forum of debate. On the first two issues, the debate will move to the courts of law. On the third issue, the debate will move to public platforms. The last word has not been said on the three issues.

PRIVACY IS THE CORE OF PERSONAL LIBERTY

10 September 2017

Judgements delivered by Indian courts invariably record the arguments of counsel for the parties to the case. In the Privacy case (*Justice K.S. Puttaswamy*), decided by the Supreme Court on 24 August 2017, the judgement of Justice Rohinton Nariman has (helpfully for the public) recorded the arguments in paragraphs 6 to 10. Let me quote from paragraph 6 of that judgement:

> 6. Appearing on behalf of the Union of India, Shri K.K. Venugopal, learned Attorney General (AG) of India, has argued that the conclusions arrived at in the 8-Judge Bench and the 5-Judge Bench decisions should not be disturbed as they are supported by the fact that the founding fathers expressly rejected the right to privacy being made part of the fundamental rights chapter of the Constitution...

In paragraphs 7, 8, 9 and 10, it was noted that the counsel for the states of Madhya Pradesh, Maharashtra, Gujarat and Haryana adopted the arguments of the AG and added their own reasons as well: concept of privacy was inherently vague, subjective, inchoate, unsound, etc.

It does not require deductive logic to conclude that the central government and BJP-ruled states took a common position that was decided upon by the BJP's leadership: that right to privacy was not, and should not be declared, a fundamental right.

The Verdict and the Spin

In the end, the Supreme Court, in a unanimous verdict (9–0), rejected these arguments. The Court held that privacy was a sound concept, that right to privacy was a fundamental right, and that the two earlier judgements were wrong and hence overruled. It was a comprehensive rejection of the arguments of the central government and BJP-ruled state governments.

After the verdict was delivered, the BJP gave it a spin. The central government, through its minister of law, no less, claimed that the Court had accepted the government's stand and the government welcomed the judgement! The nine honourable judges who heard the case would have blanched. Mr Ravi Shankar Prasad deserves an award for bravery or, at least, a place in the Indian cricket team!

The player on the government's team who emerged with credibility was Mr Mukul Rohatgi, the former AG. In a candid interview, he said had he still been in office as AG, he would have admitted that the government had lost the case. He also said that, in his opinion, the judgement of the Court was wrong.

Exploring 'Dark Matter'

Declaring a right not explicitly listed in Part III of the Constitution as a fundamental right is not unprecedented. The judgement of Justice D.Y. Chandrachud listed the precedents:

- the right to go abroad;
- the right against solitary confinement;
- the right of prisoners against various fetters;
- the right to legal aid;
- the right to speedy trial;
- the right against handcuffing;

- the right against custodial violence;
- the right against public hanging;
- the right to doctor's assistance at government hospitals;
- the right to shelter;
- the right to a healthy environment;
- the right to compensation for unlawful arrest;
- the right to freedom from torture;
- the right to reputation; and
- the right to earn a livelihood.

Justice J. Chelameswar described the exercise as exploring 'the Constitution's dark matter'. Just as it was exposited in *Kesavananda Bharati vs State of Kerala* that the Constitution had a basic structure which was beyond the power of amendment, in *Justice K.S. Puttaswamy*, the Court has discovered another gem—that the right to privacy is an inalienable part of the right to life and personal liberty (Article 21).

Through Lens of Privacy

The implications are far-reaching. Every action of the government that affects a person/citizen must now be examined through the lens of the right to privacy. The immediate candidate for questioning is linking Aadhaar to a number of activities like income tax return, PAN, bank account, air ticket, school admission, etc. That was not—repeat, not—the original purpose of Aadhaar and is, arguably, an invasion of privacy.

Aadhaar was conceived and implemented (cautiously) to ensure that government benefits and subsidies did not go into the hands of the wrong person as a result of duplication, impersonation or falsification. Cases of ghost students receiving scholarships, bogus muster rolls under MGNREGA, second or multiple subsidized LPG cylinders obtained under duplicate/multiple identities, etc., were common. Insistence on Aadhaar would put an end to the malpractices. However, under the NDA government, Aadhaar has exceeded its original purpose and has been made mandatory for activities that do not involve government benefits or subsidies. The question is, why?

The Unique Identification Authority of India (UIDAI) and its claim of data security must come under scrutiny. The National Intelligence Grid's authority and mandate must be reviewed. The powers of search and seizure, telephone tapping, off-site surveillance, etc., have to be restricted. Section 377, IPC, must be struck down (not just read down). Lesbian, gay, bisexual, and transgender (LGBT) rights need to be acknowledged. 'Know Your Customer', data-collection, data-mining, data-sharing and profiling must be regulated. 'Right to be Forgotten' must be made enforceable. Right to die, euthanasia and reproductive rights must be debated.

Justice K.S. Puttaswamy has enlarged and enriched the freedom that we won in 1947. Today, we will celebrate. Tomorrow, there will be other challenges and those too we shall overcome.

JAMMU & KASHMIR

In 2016, I had written extensively on Jammu & Kashmir. Continuing in the same vein, I wrote two columns in 2017. I braved the charge of the government (made by a minister) that I was anti-national. An attempt was made to stir a controversy during the election in Gujarat, but it did not succeed. There is a deceptive calm in J&K. There is also the distraction of a Special Representative who has been unable to speak to any of the stakeholders who matter. I expect to write more often on J&K in 2018.

KASHMIR IS SLIDING INTO DISASTER

16 April 2017

I have written many times on the situation in J&K with particular reference to the situation in the Kashmir Valley. There were five columns between April and September 2016. The thrust of my argument was, thanks to the policies adopted by the PDP–BJP government in J&K and the central government, we were losing Kashmir. Few outside the Kashmir Valley supported me; many criticized me; and a minister of the central government came close to calling me anti-national!

I have not changed my views. Rather, recent events have strengthened my views and I intend to articulate them more forcefully. My argument can be summarized thus:

Article 370 is a Compact

J&K, then ruled by a king, acceded to India in 1947 under a 'grand bargain'. Article 370 of the Constitution of India, adopted in 1950, embodied that grand bargain. Over the years, that Article has been honoured more in the breach than in the observance. The three regions of J&K have responded in different ways. The centre of the conflict is the Kashmir Valley that is home to seven million people. The people of the Valley, especially the youth, have reacted aggressively to the denial of the autonomy that was promised when J&K acceded to India. Among the people, a very small number wants the Valley to become part of Pakistan. A number of persons have turned militants and taken to violence but, at the worst of times, that number did not exceed a few hundred. The overwhelming majority, though, demands *azaadi*.

India, rather the Indian *establishment*, has reacted predictably. Every government in J&K and every government at the Centre has responded to the challenge with more warnings, more troops and more laws. I have concluded that Kashmir is one subject on which the prime minister's writ does not run. I believe Mr Atal Bihari Vajpayee genuinely looked for a resolution, spoke of *insaaniyat* (humanity), but Operation Parakram was the legacy of his government. Dr Manmohan Singh had an acute sense of history, he accommodated new ideas like the Round Table conferences, amending the Armed Forces (Special Powers) Act (AFSPA) and deploying interlocutors, but ultimately deferred to the 'establishment' view. Mr Narendra Modi surprised all by inviting Mr Nawaz Sharif to the swearing-in of the new government but soon enough he embraced the 'establishment' view.

The Worst of Times

The people of the Kashmir Valley have alternated between hope and despair. J&K has seen good times and bad times, but the present time seems to be the worst of times.

The slide to chaos began in July 2016 with the killing of Burhan Wani. That was only the immediate trigger, the seeds had been sown earlier. In 2014, after the election to the J&K Legislative Assembly, two unlikely partners, the PDP and the BJP, formed a coalition government. That was, and remains, a grave provocation. The PDP is seen as a betrayer and the BJP is seen as the usurper. Pulled in opposite directions, the state government has remained passive and helpless while the armed forces have implemented a muscular policy to quell dissent and disturbance.

Since July 2016 and up to 20 January 2017, the violence in J&K had claimed 75 lives. Besides, 12,000 people were injured, 1,000 lost vision in one eye due to pellet injuries and five were blinded (as per a report in *The Indian Express*).

As I write this, the situation in J&K has worsened. There were two by-elections—in Srinagar and Anantnag constituencies. Srinagar constituency, spread over three districts, went to the polls on 9 April. The voter turnout was 7.14 per cent, the lowest in 28 years. There was widespread stone-pelting. Eight people were killed in police firing. Re-polling in 38 booths took place on 13 April, no voter turned up in 20 of those 38 booths, and the voting percentage in the re-poll was 2.02 per cent. Meanwhile, polling in Anantnag constituency was postponed to 25 May. The non-vote is actually a vote of no confidence against the state government and the central government.

The writing on the wall is clear. The alienation of the people of the Kashmir Valley is nearly complete. We are on the brink of losing Kashmir. We cannot retrieve the situation through a 'muscular' policy—tough talk by ministers, dire warnings from the Army Chief, deploying more troops and killing more protesters.

A Last Opportunity

At the risk of being labelled anti-national, let me list the first few steps that must be taken:

1. Ask the PDP–BJP government to resign and promulgate Governor's Rule. Mr N.N. Vohra has done a great job as governor, but it is time for a new governor.
2. Announce that the central government will begin a dialogue with all the stakeholders. Talks can begin with civil society groups and student leaders. Eventually, talks must be held with the separatists.
3. Appoint interlocutors to pave the way for talks.
4. Reduce the presence of the Army and paramilitary forces and hand over the responsibility of maintaining law and order in the Kashmir Valley to the J&K police.
5. Defend the border with Pakistan by all means, take deterrent

action against infiltrators on the border, but put on hold 'counter-terrorist operations' in the Valley.

If the current medicine of tough talk and tougher action has not worked in J&K, why is it not opportune to try an alternative cure?

PUSHING EACH OTHER TO THE BRINK

16 July 2017

On many occasions in the past, I had cautioned that the Kashmir issue or problem (or by whatever name it is called) was a festering wound. Every government in the past had, in different degrees, recognized that the festering wound had to be attended to. The agreement between Jawaharlal Nehru and Sheikh Abdullah, the Tashkent agreement, the Simla Agreement, the agreement between Indira Gandhi and Sheikh Abdullah, the Agra summit, and the Lahore Declaration were, among others, genuine attempts to find a permanent solution to different aspects of the issue. None of the attempts, however, succeeded in finding a permanent solution. All outcomes left one or more stakeholders dissatisfied. The wound continued to fester.

Of the stakeholders, the most difficult, unpredictable and intractable were the young men who took to militancy. The other stakeholders had at different times shown different degrees of reasonableness.

Maximalist Positions

The central government—under every party and every prime minister—had always attempted to reach out to one or more stakeholders. I am afraid that the position of the central government seems to have decisively changed since the year 2015–16. The current central government has to be described, regretfully, as equally difficult; its rhetoric is unpredictable, and only time will tell if it is also intractable.

Just as the militants have taken a maximalist position that has to be rejected out of hand, the central government has taken a maximalist position that has aggravated the problem. The people of the Kashmir Valley are caught between the two maximalist positions. As a result, with every passing day, the security and political situation in J&K has worsened. Facts stare at our face:

	2017 (Until 30 June)	**2016**
Security forces killed	40	30
Civilians killed	28	5
Militants killed	92	77
Infiltrations	124	90

What Has Changed

Earlier, young men came out into the streets and pelted stones; now young women are also coming out into the streets. Earlier, parents restrained their children; now, a mother says (as one mother actually said), 'I cannot ask my child not to join the protesters because he believes that he is fighting for his future and his freedom.'

Earlier, the central government and the J&K government tried to be on the same page and to speak the same language. That was so even if two parties were not in a coalition. Today, the central government and the J&K government have taken diametrically opposite positions though the two parties (the BJP and PDP) pretend to run a coalition government in the state!

Earlier, the central government and the J&K government had the same view on deployment of security forces. Today, the two parties (the BJP and PDP) are daggers drawn on the question of deployment of security forces.

Earlier, the Unified Command meetings were chaired by the chief minister of J&K and his view was usually decisive. Today, although the chief minister chairs the infrequent meetings of the Unified Command, it is the view of the Army, represented by the Northern Army Command, that is decisive.

Earlier, if talks were held with any stakeholder, the central government and the J&K government supported such talks. Today, the J&K government advocates talks with all stakeholders (including Pakistan and Hurriyat) while the central government is implacably opposed to talks with any stakeholder.

Earlier, except on one occasion, Amarnath *yatris* (pilgrims) were safe. That was so for nearly 15 years. Today, the Amarnath *yatris* do not enjoy that comfort and the terrorist incident of 10 July 2017 has put in question the capacity of the government to secure the *yatris*. The Deputy Chief Minister of the state (a BJP leader) has admitted to security lapses.

It is useful to remember that fatalities in violence by terrorists hit a peak of 4,507 in 2001 before declining to 2,542 in 2003. Thereafter, it declined dramatically to 117 in 2012 and 181 in 2013. That story seems to have changed.

On the two sides of the present aggravated situation of confrontation are the militants and the BJP-led central government. I am afraid that the maximalist position that each one has taken is pushing the other to the brink and further hardening the positions of both. The casualties are the people of J&K (especially those in the Valley) and the future of the state.

Permanent Solution or Permanent Disruption

The responsibility for the present acute crisis lies on three parties: (1) the militants and their masters, undoubtedly terrorists, who will never succeed in snatching the Valley from India; (2) the BJP-led central government that believes in a military solution and has no understanding of history or of the complexities of conflict-resolution; and (3) the PDP that has shamelessly surrendered every principle it had stood for under Mufti Mohammad Sayeed and clings to office as a vassal of the BJP.

The odd man out is the home minister who makes intriguing statements like 'we have found a permanent solution to the Kashmir issue'. Will he please tell the nation what it is and what his government has done to achieve that permanent solution?

Nothing that we say or write will change the hard (and wrong) position of the militants; they have to be defeated by the strength of our security forces. But if nothing that we say or write will change the hard (and wrong) position of our government, it appears that we are on course not to a permanent solution but to a permanent disruption.

GUJARAT

The defining political event of 2017 was the intriguing verdict in the election to the Gujarat legislature. The BJP won the election but was dejected. The Congress lost the election but was rejuvenated. Such are the glorious uncertainties of elections. Will the BJP and the government change course is the question. The winter session of Parliament was as acrimonious as ever. Both sides seem to be preparing for the next round of elections in four Northeastern states and Karnataka.

DEVELOPMENT, AND THOSE LEFT BEHIND

19 November 2017

Development means different things to different people. After contesting from a largely rural parliamentary constituency for more than 30 years, I often recount the following true story.

Thirty years ago, many villages in Sivaganga were not connected by a road. The constant refrain was 'get us a road'. Under one programme or other, the administration would find the money to make a 'formation road', usually a mud road. The people were happy that development had come. A couple of years later, they would be dissatisfied, point to the state of the road after the monsoons, and demand a gravel road. The story would be repeated once every two or three years: first a road, then a gravel road, then a metal road, then a black-topped (tar) road, and then a road laid and paved using a machine.

I have learned from experience that while people took pride when India joined the nuclear club or sent a Mission to Mars, development came to the people through the satisfaction of their immediate and material needs—water, electricity, schools, primary health centres, roads, industries, jobs, prices for agricultural produce and so on. Ultimately, development concerned the quality of life, longevity, good health, good education and greater income.

Sense of Disappointment

Mr Narendra Modi, the candidate, claimed to bring development to the centre of the political debate in 2014 with his brilliant slogan *achhe din aane wale hain* (good days are coming). He also took to grandstanding with his extravagant promises: 'I will create two crore jobs every year', 'I will bring back black money stashed abroad and put ₹15 lakh in the bank account of every Indian', and so on. Obviously, none of the extravagant promises could be fulfilled. Hence, the all-round sense of disappointment after 42 months.

A similar sense of disappointment prevails in Gujarat which goes to election in December. The much-touted 'Gujarat Model' is being dissected and examined. The best thing that happened to Gujarat was the formation of the state in 1960. In the 57 years since, Gujarat has been ruled by the Congress (and by some offshoots) in the first three decades and by the BJP since 1995. Even before 1995, Gujarat's growth rate was higher than the national average and Gujarat has maintained that edge. Amul, the ports, the vibrant textile industry and the chemical and petrochemical industry predate 1995. A large share of the credit is due to the people of Gujarat. (Basically, Gujaratis are a mercantile community. They are focused on trade and business.)

Distributive Justice

Where the government of Gujarat has faltered—and can be faulted—is in its neglect of distributive justice. We may compare Gujarat with its sibling Maharashtra as well as with other frontline states like Karnataka and Tamil Nadu. Kerala, with its outstanding gains in Human Development Index (HDI), is another comparable state (see Table on the following page).

Sr.	Indicator	Gujarat	Maharashtra	Kerala	Karnataka	Tamil Nadu
1	HDI Rank	11	7	1	12	8
2	Literacy (2011)	79.31%	82.9%	94.0%	75.6%	80.33%
3	Life Expectancy in Years (2011–15)	69.1	72.0	75.2	69.0	71.0
4	Infant Mortality (per 1,000 live births) (National Family Health Survey [NFHS]-4)	30	19	10	24	17
5	Sex Ratio (females/1000 males)	918	925	1,084	973	995
6	Children					
(6a)	Underweight	39.3%	36%	16.1%	35.2%	23.8%
(6b)	Stunted	38.5%	34.4%	19.7%	36.2%	27.1%
(6c)	Fully Immunized	50.4%	56.3%	82.1%	62.6%	69.7%
7	Poverty Ratio (Rangarajan Committee)	27.4%	20.0%	11.3%	21.9%	22.4%
8	Gross Enrolment Ratios for Secondary Schools (2015–16)	74.13%	89.95%	102.44%	83.22%	93.92%
9	Social Sector Expenditure in ₹crore (2016–17)	61,960	122,604	40,592	66,659	78,180
(9a)	Per Capita Social Sector Expenditure (₹)	7,819	7,859	8,535	8,430	8,698

The Table tells the story of Gujarat and how, despite the boasts, Gujarat is not ahead of four comparable states. While Gujarat has progressed industrially, in many critical areas of human development, it may have actually regressed in the last 22 years. The most shocking statistics concern the children. It is because of the neglect of the social sector and an apparent disdain for the poor.

Social Mobilization

As a result of a distorted concept of development or *vikas*, many sections of the people have been left behind. They are mainly the Scheduled Tribes (14.8 per cent of the population), Dalits (7.1 per cent) and the minorities (11.5 per cent). Even the Patel community (Patidars) is unhappy because they have not been put under the Other Backward Classes category and believe they have lost out on jobs and educational opportunities. There is massive social mobilization: caste is an easier vehicle to mobilize, but the real motivation is absence of jobs. The slogan that has gone viral is *vikas gando thayo che* (Development has gone crazy!).

Any observer of Gujarat will notice the ferment in the society. The fault lines are visible. Many people openly say 'change is in the air'. The election in Gujarat promises to be a contest of many hues: Economic/ Social Reality vs Headline Grabbing Announcements and Poor Human Development Indicators vs Billion Dollar Investment Proposals.

It may turn out to be an absorbing contest of Young Aspirational Leaders vs Old Warhorses.

THE SONS OF THE SOIL OF GUJARAT

3 December 2017

The prime minister began his election campaign in Bhuj, Gujarat, proclaiming that he was the 'son of Gujarat', and warned that anyone who comes to Gujarat and levels allegations against the son of the soil will not be forgiven by the people of the state.

The BJP has ruled Gujarat since 1995. Mr Modi became the chief minister in October 2001 and, after he vacated the office in 2014, the state has had two chief ministers hand-picked by him. The first (Ms Anandiben Patel) was a disaster and the second (Mr Vijay Rupani) is a disappointment. Hence the need for Mr Modi to make himself the election issue and ask for votes in his name. I think it is unusual for a prime minister to do so.

Gujarat Not Exceptional

In the last 57 years, Gujarat, like other states, has made progress. It is one of the states that benefited from the liberalization of 1991, but Gujarat is not exceptional. In September 2013, a committee under Dr Raghuram Rajan constructed an 'Underdevelopment Index' for 28 states for the purpose of evolving a method for allocation of central funds. The least developed state was Odisha with an index of 0.79 and the most developed states were Goa (0.05) and Kerala (0.15). Gujarat got an index of 0.50, in the midpoint of the scale, and was almost on a par with Karnataka. On the Social Progress Index for 29 states, released by the Institute for Competitiveness and the Social Progress Imperative, Gujarat is plumb in the middle (rank 15) with 14 states above and 14 states below. Gujarat is in the top five on 'Basic Human Needs' but in the bottom five on 'Foundations of Wellbeing' and ninth from the bottom on 'Opportunity'.

People Have Grievances

Like in every state, sections of the people of Gujarat are dissatisfied. The farmers are particularly unhappy. The Sardar Sarovar Dam is an example of poor governance. Less than a quarter of the planned 18.45 lakh hectares receives water for irrigation. Over 30,000 km of canals are yet to be completed. Mr Tushaar Shah, a senior fellow at the International Water Management Institute, writes: 'After 35 years in the works, ₹48,000 crore in capex, 45,000 ousted families, 245 submerged villages and 250,000 hectares of land acquired, for Gujarat, the Sardar Sarovar Dam project still remains just that, a promise.'

Other sections of the people have their own grievances. The Patidars want reservation for their community in jobs and educational institutions. The Dalits and the Scheduled Tribes believe they have been neglected and are the victims of oppression and violence. The minorities believe they are discriminated against and a majoritarian agenda is being imposed upon them.

There are voices in Gujarat in support of and against demonetisation. There are people who are tolerant of the flawed implementation of the GST as well as people—particularly in the MSME sector, textile business and diamond trade—who are indignant at the faulty design and hasty implementation of the GST. New appointees among Gujarat's government servants, including teachers, are contract employees on low, fixed salaries—a clear violation of Article 14.

Such grievances are not peculiar to Gujarat. Movements, organizations and leaders will emerge to voice the grievances. That is the way a democracy works. Mr Hardik Patel, Mr Jignesh Mevani and Mr Alpesh Thakor have emerged as leaders. They are entitled to oppose the government of the day and to ask for the support of the people. They and the farmers, traders and government servants have not 'come to Gujarat' to level allegations against a son of the soil. They are as much sons of the soil as Mr Narendra Modi is.

Real Issues Ignored

Mr Modi is prime minister of India. He promised *achhe din*. He promised to bring back the black money stashed abroad and deposit ₹15 lakh in the bank account of every person. He promised two crore jobs every year. He should speak on those promises. He should speak on the concerns of the people of Gujarat, on Sardar Sarovar Dam, on Una, on the ghettoization of towns and cities, on the financial condition of Gujarat State Petroleum Corporation, on the Nano car project, on malnourished children, on the sex ratio and on the flourishing illegal trade in liquor.

He should speak on matters that concern all of India, such as farmers' distress, oppression of Dalits, discrimination against minorities, deprivation of forest and other rights of the Scheduled Tribes, unemployment, price rise, plight of MSMEs, reservation, majoritarianism, intolerance, vigilantism, the Rafale deal and the GDP growth rate.

Nobody has hurt Gujarati *asmita* (pride). No one hates Gujarat or Gujaratis. Long before Mr Modi became chief minister, the Indian people and the central governments (including Congress governments) had recognized the achievements of numerous Gujaratis, starting with Mahatma Gandhi. Gandhiji was an Indian and a son of Gujarat; he is revered as the Father of the Nation; and his chosen instrument to lead the freedom struggle was the Congress party. Jawaharlal Nehru and Sardar Patel were comrades-in-arms and remained so until the Sardar's untimely death. Morarji Desai, Gulzarilal Nanda, Vikram Sarabhai, Jhaverchand Meghani, Tribhuvandas Patel, I.G. Patel and many others—besides Gujarati-speaking Parsis—were honoured and celebrated citizens.

Even during a state election, Mr Narendra Modi should speak as the prime minister of India.

GUJARAT AFTER 22 YEARS OF BJP RULE

10 December 2017

A social media commentator has claimed to have analysed the recent election speeches of Prime Minister Narendra Modi in 29 rallies and found that Mr Rahul Gandhi got 621 mentions, the Congress 427 mentions and the Gujarat Model none! This may be an exaggeration or simply bad counting but it highlights an important aspect of the BJP's campaign in Gujarat: The campaign has not been about *vikas* or *achhe din*. It has been about the alleged bad days of the Congress. One could not have encountered a more negative campaign from the ruling party.

The Congress was last in office in Gujarat in 1995. At the Centre, the Congress's term ended in May 2014. The election in Gujarat is not about Mr Rahul Gandhi or the Congress, it is about what successive BJP governments since 1995 have delivered to the people of Gujarat. It is about the present needs and anxieties and fears of the people of Gujarat.

Price Rise and Development

Available reports and evidence indicate that the top four issues on the minds of the voters of Gujarat are price rise (18 per cent), development (13 per cent), unemployment (11 per cent) and poverty (11 per cent). No one from the ruling party will speak on price rise. It was left to the RBI to frame the issue and address it. And this is what the RBI said on 5 December 2017: 'Inflation may continue to accelerate in the near term... The recent rise in international crude oil prices may sustain... Any adverse supply shock due to geopolitical developments could push prices up even further.'

For three years, the central government reaped a windfall due to low crude oil prices but stubbornly refused to heed the demand to cut retail prices of petrol and diesel and give some relief to the consumers. The demand has got shriller, there is an obvious solution, but the government, given the state of its finances, is petrified. The obvious solution is to bring petroleum products under the GST. If I was a voter in Gujarat, I would vote for the party that promised to bring petroleum products under the GST and cut prices of petrol and diesel by at least ₹10 per litre immediately.

No one from the ruling party will speak on development and, if they do, it will be about the Bullet Train that 90 per cent of the people will never board. Or it will be about the Sardar Sarovar Dam whose waters cannot be distributed to water-starved Saurashtra and other districts because the bulk of the canal network (30,000 km) has not been built in the last 22 years. No wonder the people of Gujarat say *vikas gando thayo che*. If I was a voter in Gujarat, I would vote for the party that promised to quickly complete the Sardar Sarovar canal network, build highways and all-weather roads, repair and maintain city roads, and construct airports in every region.

Unemployment and Poverty

No one from the BJP will speak on unemployment. The BJP will point to the low number of persons registered with employment exchanges. That is a self-goal. There is widespread unemployment and there is no hope that one will get a job by registering with employment exchanges. Add to that the fact that thousands of persons lost their jobs (in Gujarat and elsewhere) due to demonetisation and the throttling of MSMEs by a flawed GST. It is not difficult to understand why thousands of youth are rallying behind Gujarat's intrepid young leaders. If I was a voter in

Gujarat, I would vote for the party that will fill the thousands of vacant posts in the government (and pay fair wages, not fixed amounts) and incentivize MSMEs to grow and create jobs.

The BJP government in Gujarat has turned its back on the poor. How else can one explain the disappointing human development indicators or why Gujarat ranks behind many states in child health, literacy, sex ratio and per capita social sector expenditure? If I was a voter in Gujarat, I would vote for the party that will empathize with the poor and the middle class and pledge its time and resources to address their real problems irrespective of religion or caste.

Election and Accountability

I shall readily admit that the issues of development and jobs and price rise are common to all states. In the past too, ruling parties attempted to sidestep the real issues, but wise voters changed the government, and with every election the voters have become wiser.

The debate that the BJP wants to stir is on Hindutva, Ayodhya, personal laws, cow protection, hyper-nationalism and the fault lines in society. The prime minister, in his speeches, will invariably pick one or more of these subjects and make a remark that will become the headline of the day. The media will start a raucous debate. Thankfully, so far, no party has walked into that trap. They have remained focused on development and on the issues of jobs and price rise.

No one can predict the result of an election. Bihar went contrary to surveys; Uttar Pradesh went contrary to opinion polls. We can only hope that, for the sake of Gujarat and for the sake of better governance at the Centre in the next 16 months, the voters of Gujarat will remember that an election is the time to enforce accountability.

GUJARAT WINNER AND ECONOMY ARE LIMPING

24 December 2017

In 'Now, Return to Governance', my column dated 17 December 2017, I had written that 'the [BJP] may still ride to victory' in Gujarat. As it turned out, the BJP did not 'ride to victory'. The BJP limped across the finish line with a young and energized sprinter close on its heels. Both the BJP and the Congress were winners: the BJP scored an electoral victory, the Congress scored a political victory. The BJP's leadership has reason to be despondent that it lost 16 seats (from the 115 seats it had held) and was nowhere near its declared goal of 150 seats. The Congress's leadership has reason to be disappointed because it came so near (80 seats) but couldn't cross the finish line (92 seats).

Incumbent and Challenger

The takeaways from the election in Gujarat are many. I shall list a few:

1. The BJP under the leadership of Mr Narendra Modi is not unbeatable. Delhi and Bihar were not flashes in the pan or flukes. A strong narrative and a carefully-crafted strategy can defeat the BJP.
2. Vote swings can be very large between one election and another even if the interval is only two or three years.

3. In Gujarat, the critical factor was not *caste* but *mobilization.* Such mobilization can take place around other factors as well—joblessness or farmers' distress or growing inequality or religion. The outreach of social movements can be larger than the reach of political parties and may determine the outcome of an election.
4. Mr Rahul Gandhi has his task cut out. He has galvanized the Congress' cadres but their numbers must increase and they must be welded into organizational units. The 'missing' organizational units may explain the difference between 80 seats and 92 seats.
5. Mr Narendra Modi has to deliver on his promises—growth, jobs, doubling farm income, and *sabka saath, sabka vikas.* The first three years of his government have returned an average growth rate of 7.5 per cent (under the new methodology). That is a long distance away from the double-digit growth that was promised. Jobs are not in sight. Doubling farm income—I suppose real income—seems to be a pipe dream. *Sabka saath* is belied by the divisiveness and hate spread by the BJP/RSS's foot soldiers and even some leaders.

Economy and Jobs

Ultimately, it is the state of the economy in 2018–19 that will be the decisive factor in the elections over the next 16 months, including the Lok Sabha election. In 'economy', the critical factor will be 'jobs'. Hence, it makes sense to talk about the outlook for the economy and for employment.

The last exposition on the economy by an official source was by the RBI at the last Monetary Policy Review on 6 December 2017. After noting that manufacturing, mining and electricity, gas, water supply, etc., (constituting 'Industry') accelerated in Q2 of 2017–18, the RBI pointed out that:

> In contrast, growth in agriculture and allied activities slackened, reflecting the lower than expected *kharif* harvest. Activity in the services sector decelerated, mainly on account of slowdown in

financial, insurance, real estate and professional services, and in public administration, defence and other services (PADO) following the large front-loading of government expenditure in Q1. Despite some improvement, construction sector growth remained tepid due to transitory effects of the RERA and GST implementation. Growth in the trade, hotels, transport and communication sub-group remained resilient, in spite of some slowdown in growth in Q2 as compared with the previous quarter. On the expenditure side, the growth of gross fixed capital formation improved for the second successive quarter. However, growth in private final consumption expenditure—the mainstay of aggregate demand—slowed to an eight-quarter low in Q2.

If growth in agriculture *slackened*, services sector *decelerated*, construction sector was *tepid*, growth in trade, hotels, etc., *slowed down*, and growth in private final consumption expenditure *slowed* to an eight-quarter low, will anyone in his right senses say that the economy is healthy?

MUDRA and Myth

Let us look at just one boast of the government—that millions of jobs were created in the last three years. On 28 March 2016, the prime minister referred to the MUDRA (Micro Units Development and Refinance Agency Ltd.) scheme and said, 'over 31 million loans have been sanctioned to entrepreneurs... Even if we assume conservatively that, on average, each enterprise creates just one sustainable job, this initiative itself amounts to 31 million in new employment.'

MUDRA loans are simply an aggregate of loans given by public sector banks and regional rural banks—what they have been doing for many years. As on 28 July 2017, 8.56 crore loans had been sanctioned. The total amount was ₹3.69 lakh crore. The average loan size was ₹43,000!

We are asked to believe that a loan of ₹43,000 will create an additional job! If the 'new' worker is paid less-than-minimum wage of ₹5000 a month, the loan will evaporate in eight months! Can an investment of

₹43,000 generate additional income of ₹5000 per month?

The claim that every loan created 'one sustainable job' is false. It is just like the boast that ₹15 lakh will be deposited in the bank account of every person after retrieving the black money stashed abroad. If you are an unemployed youth, enjoy your ₹15 lakh deposit, take the MUDRA job, eat statistics and live happily ever after!

NATION AT LARGE

In this section you will find columns on a number of unrelated subjects that did not fall under any category. I think some of the more important columns can be found in this section. I would particularly commend to you the columns on children, the looming threat to privacy, and hunger. They are the real challenges that we must overcome, but they are usually buried in the millions of words that are written about GDP, investments, interest rates, inflation and exports. I have resolved to write more on matters that we tend to neglect.

FROM UNIVERSITY TO MEDIOCRITY

26 February 2017

There is an unwritten law that one space on this earth must be inviolate. That is the space occupied by a university.

A university is not a mere collection of buildings. It is also not a collection of colleges or centres of research. It is not constituted solely for the purpose of conferring degrees upon the young men and women who enter its portals, study subjects, and pass examinations. It is a space that is designed to nurture knowledge and freedom and beckon the children of the world to take from and give unto the reservoir of knowledge and freedom.

None Among the Best

Universities have achieved greatness not only because they had able and wise teachers, but also because they attracted intelligent and creative students. The President of Harvard University was once asked how Harvard remained a treasure house of knowledge. He replied, 'Because the freshman class brings so much knowledge and the graduating class takes away so little!'

No university in India can match Harvard or Stanford, Oxford or Cambridge, McGill or Sorbonne or even the new—reinvented—universities in China (that have forged ahead and earned their places among the top

10 or top 50 or top 100 universities). The best an Indian university has been able to achieve is to be ranked in the bracket 200 to 250. That alone should be a cause of concern.

Funding was identified as a constraint. I made what was then widely hailed as a bold move: I announced a grant of ₹100 crore from the Union Budget to the Indian Institute of Science (IISc), Bengaluru, *with no conditions attached*. You may say that it was announced on a whim. It was unprecedented. No one—not the director of IISc or the ministry concerned—had asked for the grant and, for several months, they did not know what to do with the money! In subsequent years, similar grants were made to several leading institutions. In their sesquicentennial year, the universities of Calcutta, Bombay and Madras got a grant of ₹100 crore each. I don't know if the grants helped make a visible difference.

A Broken Model

The constraints, including funding, remain and have apparently become worse. The laws that apply to the universities are outdated. Appointments of vice chancellors have been taken over by the state governments or the central government, and several appointments have been found to be atrocious. There is poor teaching and little or no research in most universities. The University Grants Commission (UGC) has become one more controller or, actually, an incompetent dispenser of favours. Professional bodies (Medical Council of India, Bar Council of India, etc.) have a decisive say in granting permissions, recognition and affiliation. State governments or committees appointed by the courts have taken over the regulation of matters such as admission of students and fees. Unlike the great universities abroad, the university administration in India does not have, exclusively, the power to regulate all matters concerning the university. Power is divided among numerous authorities and the result is the collapse of the idea of an autonomous university. What we have is another broken institution.

In recent years, we have had examples of distinguished scholars resigning in disgust, protesting against the interference of government.

We have also had examples of many dubious appointees being removed from office. Central universities, Indian Institutes of Technology (IITs) and Indian Institutes of Management (IIMs), that were once regarded as islands of comparative excellence, have become zones of conflict like any other State-run university. Even the inspiring idea of Nalanda University now lies in a shambles.

The University of Hyderabad could not handle a routine disagreement between two politically-affiliated groups of students. JNU faces an existential threat because its founding ideas are the diametric opposite of the founding ideas of the RSS–BJP dispensation. A student union leader (Mr Kanhaiya Kumar) was roughed up on the court's premises and thrown into jail on charges of sedition, though there is not a shred of evidence for invoking that colonial-era law. An invitation to a student leader (Mr Umar Khalid) by another college (Ramjas College) led to an unprovoked attack on students by self-appointed commissars of national interest (ABVP), with the police watching the mayhem.

Cry for Reform

There is no substitute for State-funded public universities if we wish to provide access to affordable higher education to a socially diverse population. At the same time, there must be ample scope for private universities that are free from government control and interference. Both models can coexist. The only common rules that must apply to both models are:

1. There must be an independent Board of Governors with clear and transparent rules for selection and appointment of members of the Board;
2. The university cannot be a for-profit institution and must reinvest its surplus in the university; and
3. The university must abide by the laws governing reservation for the socially and educationally backward classes of citizens in appointments to the faculty and admission of students.

Today, no Indian university can escape the charge of mediocrity. It is a miracle that hundreds of students are still able to acquire the rudimentary knowledge that, combined with their native intelligence and penchant for hard work, will earn them a place in a reputed foreign university that will lead to a promising career. It is unfortunate but true that the best Indian student discovers his/her best not because of the current university system but despite the broken system.

Here is an area crying for reform.

CELEBRATING GODS, NEGLECTING CHILDREN

26 March 2017

'Human resource development' is the new name for 'education'. Rajiv Gandhi's path-breaking and far-sighted idea of an all-embracing Ministry of Human Resource Development was abandoned soon after his death and what we have today is nothing different from the old Ministry of Education. Unfortunately, our idea of human resource development is minus child development, minus child health and minus child nutrition.

We seem to have forgotten that education is for the child. Education will unleash the full potential of the child only if the child is well-fed and healthy. True, we have taken a number of initiatives to educate children, but what is the state of the children we wish to educate and who we hope will bloom into fine adult citizens?

The National Family Health Survey (NFHS) 2015–16 is the fourth in the NFHS series. It provides the most comprehensive information (and data) on population, health and nutrition for the country and for each state. It is a report that is uplifting on some aspects and depressing on many others.

Shocking Results

Undoubtedly, since Independence, India has made remarkable progress in several human development indicators. For example, since 1947, life expectancy has increased from 32 years to 66 years and literacy from 12 per cent to 74 per cent. Gender disparity between males and females on several indicators has narrowed. Nevertheless, the state of our children, despite the progress, is a matter of shame.

Let's look at key indicators revealed by the NFHS 2015–16:

	NFHS 2015–16	**NFHS 2005–06**
Sex Ratio at Birth for Children Born in the Last Five Years (Females per 1,000)	919	914
Infant Mortality Rate (per 1,000)	41	57
Under-five Mortality Rate (per 1,000)	50	74
Children Aged 12–23 Months Fully Immunized (%)	62.0	43.5
Children Under 5 who are Stunted (Height for Age) (%)	38.4	48.0
Children Under 5 who are Wasted (Weight for Height) (%)	21.0	19.8
Children Under 5 who are Severely Wasted (%)	7.5	6.4
Children Under 5 who are Underweight (Weight for Age) (%)	35.7	42.5
Children Aged 6–59 Months who are Anaemic (%)	58.4	69.4

It has been medically established that the first five years of a child determine, by and large, the child's health and physical and mental development during the rest of its life. What is the state of India's children? One out of two children is anaemic, one out of three is underweight and stunted, and one out of five is wasted. The reasons are inadequate food, low nutrition, bad drinking water and appalling sanitation.

Food Security Neglected

India is a signatory to the United Nations Human Rights Commission's Convention on the Rights of the Child. Article 24 (2) of the Convention states, *inter alia*, that: 'State Parties shall…take appropriate measures to combat disease and malnutrition…through provision of adequate nutritious food and clean drinking water.'

The National Food Security Act (NFSA), 2013, was enacted for 'ensuring access to adequate quantity of quality food at affordable prices'. It promised 5 kg of grain per person per month. Special provisions were made for pregnant and lactating mothers, children aged between 6 months and 6 years, and children suffering from malnutrition. Modest nutritional standards were specified: 500 to 800 calories and 12 to 25 gm of protein per day for various categories. The law mandated a State Food Commission in every state to oversee the implementation of the Act. As on 21 March 2017, the promise of the Act remained unfulfilled; and nine state governments had not constituted the State Food Commission. The list included large states like Maharashtra, Gujarat and Karnataka and historically poor states like Chhattisgarh, Jharkhand and Odisha. The Supreme Court has summoned the chief secretaries concerned to answer charges of callous negligence.

Doubtful Commitment

While the primary responsibility lies with the state governments, the central government's commitment to our children is also suspect. Look at how little the central government spends on key areas:

	2013–14	**2014–15**	**2015–16**	**2016–17**
Ministry of Human Resource Development	4.57	4.24	3.75	3.65
Ministry of Health & Family Welfare	1.89	1.90	1.90	1.97
Ministry of Women & Child Development	1.16	1.11	0.96	0.88
Total	7.62	7.25	6.61	6.50

(as per cent of total expenditure)

If the government had maintained the expenditure in the subsequent years at the same level as in 2013–14, it would have spent an additional amount of ₹6,155 crore, ₹18,087 crore and ₹22,561 crore in the subsequent three years.

Successive governments—especially state governments—have miserably failed to look after the children of India. That, in my view, is the duty of the State next only to the duty to maintain law and order. Because of neglect, the quality of our human resources is poor. From economic growth to national security, everything depends on the quality of our human capital. The demographic dividend that we boast of is in danger of turning into a demographic millstone.

There is a proverb in Tamil to the effect, 'Child and God dwell where they are celebrated'. It is sad that, as a nation, we celebrate our gods, but we neglect our children.

GO BACK AND READ GEORGE ORWELL

23 April 2017

Aadhaar, a unique identification number to every citizen, was an idea born in 2009. Was it an idea ahead of its time? A lot of people thought so, especially people working at the ground level among the poor and those from the neglected sections.

Aadhaar was not a revolutionary idea. It is the foundation on which identity cards are issued in dozens of countries. Aadhaar was also not a novel idea. In India, other instruments have been issued—and are in use—which also serve as proof of identity for certain purposes. The best known are passports, driving licences, PAN and ration cards.

What led to the idea of Aadhaar? The government transfers a number of benefits to different sections of the people. Among them are scholarships, old-age pensions, subsidies, etc. In a vast country with a very large population, the delivery of benefits to the right persons poses a formidable challenge. Impersonation, falsification, duplication, pilferage, diversion and rent-seeking are the bane of any system of delivering benefits. Aadhaar was intended to get rid of the known evils of the system.

BJP Led the Opposition

Yet, when the idea of Aadhaar was mooted, it ran into fierce opposition. Nowhere was the opposition expressed more vehemently than in the report of the Parliamentary Standing Committee on Finance presented to both Houses of Parliament on 13 December 2011. Mr Yashwant Sinha, as Chairman of the Committee, led the charge against Aadhaar. From the pronouncements of prominent BJP leaders at that time (Mr Narendra Modi, Mr Prakash Javadekar and Mr Ananth Kumar) it was evident that Mr Sinha had the support of a powerful section of his party. Today, if he reads some of the conclusions of the Committee, he will be embarrassed!

The Yashwant Sinha-led Committee slammed almost every aspect of Aadhaar and the Bill to establish the UIDAI. It questioned the wisdom of collecting biometric information; it warned of ID fraud; it pointed out that the estimate of failure of biometrics was as high as 15 per cent; it highlighted issues of privacy and data security; it cautioned against the involvement of private agencies, etc. The Committee's most serious objection was to the possible exclusion of genuine beneficiaries and it observed: 'Although the scheme claims that obtaining Aadhaar number is voluntary, an apprehension is found to have developed in the minds of people that, in future, services/benefits including food entitlements would be denied in case they do not have Aadhaar number.'

UPA Moved Cautiously

Nevertheless, the UPA government moved forward cautiously, using its executive powers, a non-statutory UIDAI, and the impressive talent assembled by Mr Nandan Nilekani. Before the UPA demitted office, 600 million Aadhaar cards had been issued (now one billion) and some DBT schemes had been linked to Aadhaar.

Studies have indicated that DBT works: transfer of old-age pensions through DBT has reduced the incidence of poverty. Cash transfers, instead of transfer in kind, have not adversely impacted food consumption; on the contrary they have increased consumption of eggs, pulses, fish and meat. On the other hand, cash transfer instead of kerosene has increased the demand for fuelwood.

However, sections of civil society continued to challenge Aadhaar, mainly on the ground that it may have the unintended consequence of excluding deserving beneficiaries. The Supreme Court stepped in and, in 2013, by an interim order, directed that Aadhaar could not be made mandatory to receive benefits. In 2015, the Court agreed to examine issues relating to privacy and referred the case to a larger bench of the Court. Aadhaar was permitted only for DBT schemes such as scholarships, social security payments, subsidized LPG and MGNREGA wages.

On assuming office, the NDA–BJP government did a U-turn. Mr Arun Jaitley admitted as much when he said that, following a presentation by the UIDAI and satisfactory answers to questions, the government was convinced about the merit of the Aadhaar project!

While the change of heart was welcome, what one did not expect was that the government would throw all caution to the winds and extend Aadhaar, indiscriminately, to welfare as well as non-welfare programmes. The government has made the possession of Aadhaar practically mandatory to receive benefits or to comply with regulatory laws, thus brazenly disregarding the limits set by the Supreme Court. Aadhaar is now required to file an income tax return, to get a mobile telephone connection, to receive a university degree and so on. Soon, it is feared, Aadhaar will be mandatory to get a driving licence or an air ticket or even a rail ticket. Will it then be extended to taking health insurance or becoming a member of a library or paying one's club bills?

The Privacy Issue

That would be a gross and unconstitutional invasion of privacy. While a unique identity mark is necessary, it cannot become a potential device to spy on people's lives or gather private information that has no relevance to good governance. We must remember we do not yet have a comprehensive law on data protection or privacy.

Implementing an idea as far-reaching as Aadhaar requires careful design, pilot projects, testing and validation, and robust security features.

Absent these limiting factors, yet implementing Aadhaar on a mandatory basis, will give the government the instrument and the power to build a mass surveillance system and take one step towards an Orwellian State. Don't say you were not warned.

DO NOT STIR UP A HORNETS' NEST

30 April 2017

Last week, I found myself in the unenviable position of not being able to either own or disown a report of a Parliamentary Committee! Such are the challenges of holding a public office.

The Parliamentary Committee on Official Language was first constituted in 1976. By convention, the home minister is the *ex-officio* chairman of the committee. There are 20 members elected by the Lok Sabha and 10 elected by the Rajya Sabha. The 'election' is only a formal procedure, since the political parties in each House of Parliament get proportionate representation and they nominate their candidates accordingly.

Protagonists of Hindi

The object of the Committee is to promote the use of Hindi. Political parties usually nominate to the Committee protagonists of Hindi. Naturally, the members of the Committee, or at least the overwhelming majority of the members, consider it their duty to recommend measures that will accelerate the use of Hindi for all official purposes.

After I was appointed home minister in December 2008, I was designated as the chairman. Mr Satyavrat Chaturvedi, an ardent supporter of the increased use of Hindi, was the deputy chairman. The 30 members were distributed among sub-committees. The most important sub-committee was the Drafting and Evidence Sub-Committee. It was chaired by the deputy chairman.

As I recall from memory, evidence was recorded in Hindi and the report was drafted in Hindi. The full Committee adopted, after some discussion, the report. I recall that the deliberations were in Hindi and I was, for the most part, a silent and somewhat bemused listener! Obviously, the views of the overwhelming majority of the members were reflected in the recommendations contained in the report. The chairman did not have any extraordinary powers and certainly could not overrule the views of the majority, in this case an overwhelming majority. As chairman, it was my duty to submit the report to the government, which I did in 2011.

It appears that, recently, the government accepted all but a few recommendations of the Committee and submitted them to the President who, acting on the aid and advice of the Council of Ministers, accepted the recommendations. The recommendations were duly conveyed to the ministries of the central government and to the state governments. It is necessary to emphasize that they are *recommendations*.

Hindi and English Will Coexist

The publication of the report and the recommendations have stirred up a hornets' nest. While the concern is perhaps justified, there is no need to fear there will be catastrophic consequences. I shall tell you why I think so:

Firstly, Hindi and English have learnt to coexist peacefully! Hindi knows its place, English knows its place and, in some places, both share the space, giving rise to a unique conversational language called Hinglish! The peaceful coexistence is most evident where it matters, namely, in transacting government or official business: Hindi for conversation, Hinglish for discussion, English or Hindi for briefing the minister, English and Hindi for answering questions in Parliament, English for talks with foreign visitors, and English for subjects like science, technology, economics, commerce, defence and foreign affairs. Not much is likely to change as more and more participants become *functionally bilingual*.

Secondly, whether it is Hindi or English, it does not matter to the overwhelming majority of the people (over 90 per cent) who carry on their lives using just one language, their mother tongue. State and local body administrations are in the language of the state—Tamil in Tamil Nadu, Bangla in West Bengal, Punjabi in Punjab and so on. Those who migrate to another state become functionally literate in the language of that state.

Globalization and English

Thirdly, globalization has secured the place of English. The French, the Japanese and the Chinese are among those who most passionately love their language; they have accepted English and, increasingly, their youth speak the language quite fluently. Most globalizing Indians travel or migrate to English-speaking countries. The use of English will only grow in a globalizing world. Once parents recognized this, states had perforce to introduce teaching English as a subject beginning in Class 1.

Fourthly, the language used in the air, on the seas and in space is English, no matter what language is spoken on the land. This fact was brought home to me in the control room of M.V. Lagoon, a passenger ship plying between mainland India and the Lakshadweep islands. We cannot run Air Traffic Control (ATC) or the Vehicle Tracking System (VTS) or Mission Control Centres without English. (I am sure there are Hindi or Telugu or Assamese words for 'port' and 'starboard', but who uses them on a ship?)

Fifthly, the exponential growth of the media and the explosion in the number of platforms to access the media have obliged people to become functionally literate in English. The desire for information and the need to use technology have obliged people to learn functional English.

After conveying the recommendations of the Parliamentary Committee, the correct thing for the government to do is to do nothing. In the natural course, more and more people in India will become bilingual or trilingual or even multilingual. (The young Superintendent of Police of Lakshadweep is fluent in four languages that I heard her speak, maybe more!) States will promote their own language(s). English will thrive. Use of Hindi will increase at a natural pace. There is no need to start a controversy.

THE POOR SHALL NOT DREAM

23 July 2017

There is a government policy for everything. It is often gobbledygook, for example the Import-Export Policy until 1991–92.

Therefore, it was no surprise that the government and the public sector banks claimed that they had a policy on granting education loans. That was true, except that, in actual practice, the loans given by the banks were few; banks invariably insisted on collateral; and the borrowing students generally belonged to well-to-do families that could provide collateral security. The poor were shut out, absolutely and physically.

How the Poor Were Shut Out

In 2005, I took a close look at the so-called policy on education loans. I found that loans were simply not given to the poor. Among the poor, the few who got admission in a college relied on the few scholarships that were available or sold the few assets they had—usually a patch of land or bits of jewellery. Bank managements had stripped the branch managers of the power to grant education loans and insisted that the applications be sent to the regional office or the head office for appraisal and decision.

Bank managers routinely turned away an applicant on the ground that her place of residence or the place of the college did not fall within the service area of the branch. If a persevering applicant was able to cross all the hurdles, the ultimate weapon of denial was to demand collateral. In case the student was able to provide the collateral, citing some obscure rule, only a part of the amount applied for was sanctioned.

We changed that situation by deliberate and forceful intervention. As a result, the number of education loans went up, the average size of the loan went up and the total amount disbursed went up, year after year. Banks were required to empower their branches to grant education loans. Banks were forbidden to ask for collateral except in the case of a loan in excess of ₹750,000. The concept of service area was abolished. Slow but steady progress was made. Between 2007–08 and 2013–14 the average growth rate was 20 per cent.

Social, Economic Profile Changed

More than the number or the average size of the loans disbursed, the dramatic change was in the social and economic profile of the students. Thousands of first-generation learners got loans. Banks organized events at which education loans were given to wards of small farmers, agricultural labourers, Class IV government servants, daily wage earners, street vendors (of idlis, for instance) and so on. Many of the borrowers belonged to the Scheduled Castes or Other Backward Classes, many were girls. The case that is imprinted in my memory is of an itinerant, drum-rolling soothsayer (*kudu kuduppai karan*) who proudly declared that his son had got an education loan to study engineering!

When the UPA demitted office, as on 31 March 2014, the number of education loans that were outstanding was 766,314 and the amount outstanding was ₹58,551 crore. To this must be added the number of education loans that had been disbursed during the 10-year period and repaid by the borrowers. The programme had fired the dreams of hundreds of thousands of families.

Alas, that chapter seems to have drawn to a close under the NDA government. See Table on the following page:

	31-3-2014	31-3-2015	31-3-2016	31-12-2016
Number of Loans	766,314	668,889	598,187	N.A.
Amount Outstanding	58,551	61,259	68,613	N.A.
Amount as NPA	3,389	3,670	4,763	6,336

Amount in ₹crore
Source: Parliament Q&A

Wherever I go, I hear that education loans have dried up. The average growth rate in the last three years is just 5.3 per cent. When a programme winds down, the worst affected will be the poor who do not have any influence or connections. The message seems to have gone out that education loans are not a priority. The ostensible reason is that the NPA level of education loans is high. The powers that be are deaf to the argument that graduates are unable to repay the loans because they cannot find jobs in a period of jobless growth.

Once the banks got the message, they have gone after borrowers like savage moneylenders—sending 'recovery agents' (read musclemen), invoking sureties, encashing the collateral, filing suits, etc.

Resolution Only for the Rich

It is the ostensible reason that makes me angry. Assume that all the NPA accounts will be loss accounts, the total loss at the end of 31 December 2016 will be ₹6,336 crore. Compare that number with the amount at stake in the 12 corporate group accounts referred under the IBC: over ₹250,000 crore, of which over 60 per cent is NPA! When the 12 cases go through the IBC process, whatever maybe the mode of resolution, the banks are expected to take a hit of at least 30–50 per cent of the total amount.

Twelve promoter groups will cause the banks a humongous loss of ₹75,000 to ₹125,000 crore. That will be called 'financial resolution', the promoters will lose their equity in the company, but lending will resume to the groups. At its *worst*, the thousands of families that took education loans will cause the banks a loss of ₹6,336 crore (or let's stretch it to ₹10,000 crore). There is no resolution plan for such loans; any plan will be called 'financial catastrophe' and all education loans will be stopped. Do you see the true face of the development-cum-welfare State?

INDIA AT 70: THE CURSE OF CASTE

27 August 2017

One of the lessons that I have learned over the years is that a sense of caste superiority (or being casteist) can sit well with many virtues without the virtuous person feeling guilty or ashamed about it. Among the caste conscious were—and are—academics, writers, professionals and political leaders.

For example, few could match C. Rajagopalachari ('Rajaji') in terms of scholarship, intellect and selfless service. He was a natural choice as chief minister of Madras, as the state was then called. He was a great administrator, yet he stumbled on an issue that had a direct connection to caste. He advocated 'vocational training' as part of the school curriculum but, instead of leaving the choice of skill/trade to the student based upon his aptitude, Rajaji pushed for the student to follow the trade or occupation of his father. Rajaji's scheme was quickly dubbed *kula kalvi* or caste-based education, the ruling Congress party revolted, and he was forced to resign. (Rajaji had erred, but I do not believe he was casteist.)

Unbreachable Divisions

The origins of the Indian caste system lie in varna. Varna is the fourfold division among Hindus—Brahmin, Kshatriya, Vaishya and Sudra. The lines that divided them were horizontal, hierarchical and unbreachable:

once you were born in a Brahmin or Kshatriya or Vaishya or Sudra family, you will remain there for your life and your progeny will remain there for the duration of their lives. Nothing could be more offensive to an individual's self-worth and dignity. Buddhism and Jainism were born out of a revolt against the unbreachable divisions in the Hindu religion.

If varna was bad, jati or caste made the system worse. Within each varna there were divisions and subdivisions and each one of them came to represent a caste or a sub-caste. Each caste or sub-caste became a closed shop, it framed its own tyrannical rules, and violations were punished by exclusion or expulsion.

The worst form of caste oppression was untouchability. An 'untouchable'—now called a Dalit—was totally excluded from Hindu society. He was not only *lower* than the Sudra, the lowest in the varna hierarchy, he was actually *outside* Hindu society. His role was to serve those who belonged to the varna hierarchy, to fill lower-order occupations like cobbler and undertaker, and to do the 'unclean' jobs such as scavenging and skinning carcasses. Of course, the Dalits were also a source of cheap farm labour for the other castes.

Revolt and Support

By any standard, varna, caste and untouchability made Hindu society one of the most oppressive, exploitative and less productive social systems in the world. Note the words 'less productive': if millions were denied access to education, fair wages, right to property, social mobility and political representation, how could that society achieve its full economic potential?

Some of these issues were brought to the fore during the freedom struggle. Babasaheb Ambedkar emerged as the authentic voice of the Dalits. E.V. Ramasamy ('Periyar') took up the cause of the non-Brahmin castes: in Tamil Nadu, the non-Brahmins constituted nearly 97 per cent of the Hindu population! Sri Narayana Guru worked to liberate and unite the so-called lower castes, especially the Ezhava.

The goal of freedom absorbed the nation's attention, and social reform remained in the background. The leaders were true patriots, willing to sacrifice everything, including their lives, in the cause of freedom. Their sole weakness, it appears in retrospect, was allegiance to caste. Christophe Jaffrelot, in an illuminating article ('Defenders of Varna', *The Indian Express*, 4 August 2017), has quoted from the speeches of Mahatma Gandhi, Madan Mohan Malaviya, K.M. Munshi, Rajaji and Dayanand Saraswati in the 1920s and 1930s and argued that they had legitimized the varna hierarchy that was 'imbued with anti-individualistic values'. Jaffrelot has also quoted from Deendayal Upadhyaya's writings in 1965 and from a contemporary speech of Mr Yogi Adityanath.

The views of some leaders evolved and changed over time, in the cases of some other leaders the views seem to have become more regressive. Gandhiji said, 'I do not believe in caste in the modern sense. It is an excrescence and a handicap on progress'. On the other side, Mr Yogi Adityanath is quoted to have said, 'Castes play the same role in Hindu society that furrows play in farms, and help in keeping it organised and orderly'.

Centuries-old Puzzle

How and why the caste system has survived through the centuries is a puzzle. Why did the Kshatriyas and Vaishyas, who had power and money, accept the Brahmin as their superior? Why was the guru invariably a Brahmin? Is it because humans crave an associational life, that caste became a convenient association that gave a measure of physical and social security? Thanks to education and urbanization, caste may be eroding at the edges of Hindu society, but it still sits at the core of Hindu society.

Notwithstanding the Constitution of India or Articles 14, 15, 16, 17 and 21, caste and casteism survive to this day. Caste is the most dominant factor in politics, social relations and marriage. Caste has significant influence, in varying degrees, in government administration, private sector, trade and professions. There are deep caste divisions in the world of art, culture and literature.

In my view, caste is a curse that diminishes the potential of India and the Indian people. The annihilation of caste is nowhere in sight.

THE KILLED AND THE KILLERS

8 October 2017

Joan of Arc was burnt at the stake. Socrates was made to drink from the poisoned chalice. Sir Thomas More was beheaded. For their beliefs.

In recent times, five murders have shaken the conscience of the people of India. The media is focusing on who was the killer in each case. The police in the states concerned are searching for the killer(s). Some arrests have been made but the cases are nowhere near being solved. Both the media and the police are right in focusing on the killers. I have a slightly different take.

I think it is important that the people should ask the question *who was killed*. We know the name, life and work of each of the five persons who was killed but the killings will make sense only if we put all the information into a frame.

Narendra Dabholkar (1945–2013)

Narendra Dabholkar was a medical doctor. A little known fact is that he was a member of the Indian kabaddi team that played Bangladesh. What irked his detractors was he was Maharashtra's most prominent rationalist and anti-superstition activist. Dabholkar had penned more than a dozen books, edited a weekly for 16 years, founded the Maharashtra Andhashraddha Nirmoolan Samiti and trained more than 10,000 teachers on how to fight superstition and inculcate a scientific temper in students. Many years ago, he had drafted the Anti-Superstition and Black Magic Bill. The irony is an ordinance based on the draft was promulgated by the state government four days after Dabholkar was killed on 20 August 2013.

Govind Pansare (1933–2015)

Govind Pansare was a lifelong communist. He was born in a poor family, held low-paid jobs like newspaper vendor and municipal peon, became a lawyer practising labour law, and was a well-known writer who authored the Marathi language book *Who was Shivaji?*. He was the state secretary of the CPI and promoted the Shramik Nagari Sahakari Patsanstha (a cooperative bank). He ran a centre for couples who had entered into inter-caste or inter-faith marriages, and that earned him bitter criticism.

M.M. Kalburgi (1938–2015)

M.M. Kalburgi was a renowned professor, a former vice-chancellor of Kannada University at Hampi, a prolific writer and winner of the Sahitya Akademi Award in 2006. He wrote and spoke against superstition and idol worship in Hinduism and incurred the wrath of right-wing groups. A case was filed against him and U.R. Ananthamurthy in 2015 for 'offending religious sentiments' in a book that was published 18 years ago!

Gauri Lankesh (1962–2017)

Gauri Lankesh was a self-confessed Leftist and a fierce activist in support of Left causes, including pro-Naxalite causes. She helped in rehabilitating Naxalite cadres who desired to return to the mainstream. Gauri edited and published a tabloid that was anti-establishment, pro-poor and pro-Dalit, and was highly critical of right-wing and Hindutva policies. In the months prior to her murder, she had campaigned against fake news. She refused to be cowed down by threats and remained fearless until her last day.

Shantanu Bhowmick (1989–2017)

Shantanu Bhowmick was a young reporter for a TV channel telecast from Agartala, Tripura, earning about ₹6,000 per month. He is remembered as a courageous journalist who would always be the first to rush to the scene of an incident, determined to be the first to get a scoop and record live-from-ground-zero reports. Shantanu also ran a small nursery school called 'Manobik' (Bengali word, meaning humane) from his home. His last assignment was covering an agitation by the Indigenous People's Front of Tripura.

None of the above was a rich person ('rich' in the sense that is usually associated with exploiting the poor). None wielded political power or even sought political power. None held an important office at the time of the murder. None believed in violence. Three were old men, one was middle-aged and one was young.

Each one of the five was an educated person and apparently comfortable in the world of ideas and debate. Ideas should ordinarily threaten no one, but apparently they do. There are people who fear ideas and a rational debate over their ideas and rival ideas. I wonder who could resent, to the point of causing death, ideas such as anti-superstition, anti-idolatry and scientific temper? Who could be enraged by the few inter-caste and inter-faith marriages that take place in society? Who could be provoked by an avowed Leftist when there are thousands of declared communists? Who could be inimical to a young, intrepid journalist who was covering an agitation by a tribal group?

Profile of the Killer(s)

It is not difficult to construct a picture of the person or persons who probably committed these despicable murders. Almost certainly, they belong to right-wing groups. They are deeply conservative to the point of being reactionary. They resent ideas that challenge their own ideas. They question free speech and India's diversity. They are intolerant. They spread hate. They are emboldened when they are among like-minded people and take to violence—even murder—when they are in a group.

With that profile of the killer(s), 'who was killed' should have led the investigative agencies, by now, to 'who were the killers'. Names of some key suspects are common in four cases and some have been declared absconders. Meanwhile, hate and fear spread and we hang our heads in grief and shame.

HUNGER IS A SHAME

22 October 2017

It is sad that it required the publication of a report by the International Food Policy Research Institute (IFPRI) to draw attention to a problem that has been present in India for centuries and is endemic in all developing countries: hunger. It is an undeniable fact that a significant proportion of the Indian population goes hungry on many days of the year. Why should the government deny this depressing fact, unless it has developed the habit of denying anything that is an inconvenient truth?

There is no mystery in the numbers put out by the IFPRI (see Table below):

Year	India's Rank/ Number of Countries	India's Index Score
2007	94/118	25.03
2008	98/120	23.7
2009	102/121	23.9
2010	105/122	24.1
2011	108/122	23.7
2012	106/120	22.9
2013	105/120	21.3
2014	99/120	17.8

(Continued on p. 218)

(*Continued from p. 217*)

2015	93/117	29.0
2016	97/118	28.5
2017	100/119	31.4

A lower score means a better situation. Rise in score is deterioration.

Every year, some countries are added and some countries are dropped, presumably because of availability or non-availability of data. As the Table shows, this is not a material factor—over 11 years, the total number of countries considered has varied between 117 and 122, which is, statistically, insignificant. What conclusions can we draw?

- India's relative rank among the countries deteriorated between 2008 and 2011 but the score was more or less the same;
- India's relative rank and score improved significantly between 2011 and 2014; and
- there has been a significant decline in the score since 2014.

The Good and the Bad

The question that we have to ask ourselves is, why was India not able to maintain the trend of improvement that was witnessed up to 2014?

Every government since 1947 must be held responsible for the good and the bad, and so should the present government. The Global Hunger Index is calculated based on the proportion of the population that is undernourished; prevalence of wasting and stunting among children below the age of five; and the under-five mortality rate. There has been progress. Without burdening this column with numbers, the study of the period between 2006 and 2016 reveals that, as a proportion, *stunting* among children has declined; *anaemia* among women of reproductive age has declined; *low birth weight* has declined; *exclusive breastfeeding* has improved; but *wasting* among children has worsened. None of the states in India reached acceptable levels of wasting or underweight in 2016, based on the WHO cut-off rates for public health significance.

The reason for both the improvement and the deterioration is food—its availability, affordability and accessibility. People must have adequate food, everything else is secondary. India produces enough food for its people, but not all people get enough food to eat. That is the paradox. While many interventions were made—some achieved moderate success—the most decisive intervention was the passing of the National Food Security Act (NFSA), 2013.

The NFSA Promise

The NFSA declared 'entitlements' to foodgrains every month at subsidized prices. Every person in a 'priority household' will be entitled to 5 kg of foodgrain; every 'Antyodaya' household to 35 kg; every pregnant woman or lactating mother to a daily free meal during pregnancy and for six months after childbirth plus ₹6,000; every child under six years to a daily free meal; every child between six and 14 years to a free midday meal; and, in the case of non-supply of foodgrains or meals, to a food security allowance. It was intended to cover, if necessary, up to 75 per cent of the rural population and up to 50 per cent of the urban population. A State Commission would oversee the implementation of the Act in each state.

The NFSA was a bold, ambitious and obviously costly intervention. Reservations were expressed; however, the only alternative was a UBI that may have proved more expensive.

Grave Neglect

When the government changed in 2014, the NDA was obliged to implement the law. It did not. I cannot recall the prime minister making food security a mission (as he did Swachh Bharat), nor did the government propose an alternative. The NFSA was gravely neglected. In July 2017, the Supreme Court found that in many states the bodies charged with implementation had not been set up and described the situation as 'pathetic'. According to the Budget documents, the government spent ₹134,919 crore in 2015–16 under the NFSA. For 2016–17, it was

₹130,335 crore (budget expenditure) and ₹130,673 crore (revised expenditure), but the actual expenditure was only ₹105,672, as reported in May 2017. This was callous neglect and there has been no explanation.

The State of Food Security and Nutrition Report (UNICEF, 2017) states that 190 million people in India are undernourished. When the IFPRI holds a mirror to our face, it is not enough to deny the warts. Hunger in India is an ugly wart. The government of the day owes an obligation—higher than the promise of a bullet train or the 'tallest' statue or any other *jumla*—to propose a comprehensive solution to eliminate hunger and implement it.

SHE PUT THE POOR ON THE AGENDA

26 November 2017

19 November 2017 passed without a national observance. It was a sad reflection on our sense of history. It was a silent comment on the supposed neutrality of the State. It was a shame.

That day was the hundredth birth anniversary of Indira Gandhi, India's third and sixth prime minister. She was loved by many and hated by a significant number, but never ignored as long as she was alive.

Every prime minister has successes and failures. Both successes and failures have to be assessed in the backdrop of the time and the context in which they happened and the challenges that the country and the prime minister faced at that time. When Indira Gandhi became prime minister in 1966:

- two wars (1962 and 1965) had drained the country of its resources;
- there was an acute shortage of foodgrains and the country was dangerously dependent on food aid under P.L. 480;
- the Congress party's organization was very weak (and during the subsequent 24-month period the party would lose the elections in eight states).

Winning the Support of the Poor

After the unsatisfactory election result of 1967, it was Indira Gandhi, among all the leaders of the Congress, who correctly identified that the poor had deserted the Congress. The Congress had to win back the support of the poor. Indira Gandhi showed the way by putting forward a solid agenda that was entirely consistent with the then-prevailing ideology—socialism—of the Congress.

Indira Gandhi sent a 10-point programme to the Congress Working Committee. Some of the points do not accord with the liberal market economy of the present day, but I believe that the programme was justified, at that time, both economically and politically. Some points are relevant even today—e.g., provision of minimum needs, rural works programme and land reforms. The poor, who were on the periphery of the consciousness of political parties, were brought on the agenda and placed at the centre of the agenda.

Later, in the 20-point programme, Indira Gandhi addressed the concerns of the poor in a forthright manner by including clean drinking water, healthcare, education, social justice for Scheduled Castes and Scheduled Tribes, opportunities for women, environment protection, etc. Although the specific programmes have been restructured many times thereafter, the spirit of the 20-point programme has guided all subsequent governments' efforts towards poverty alleviation.

Poor Pushed to the Periphery

Indira Gandhi's concerted attack on poverty yielded dividends. The poverty ratio declined by nearly 10 percentage points to 44 per cent in 1984. The poor regarded Indira Gandhi as their protector and benefactor, and do so even today. Successive Congress governments, including the NDA government of Mr Atal Bihari Vajpayee, tried to keep the poor at the centre of their agenda.

Alas, no longer. The central government and several state governments have once again pushed the poor to the periphery. Allocations to education and healthcare, as a proportion of total expenditure, have been slashed. The MGNREGA was deplored as a 'monument to the failure of the UPA government'. In 2014–15 and 2015–16, paltry increases were made in the MSP for farm produce, thus adding to the distress among agriculturists. Bank credit is denied to SMEs. Above all, no worthwhile effort has been made in the last three years to create the jobs required for the 1.2 crore youth who enter the job market every year.

How the Poor are Cheated

Clever slogans have replaced the pro-poor agenda. Our cities are barely liveable, yet we will spend huge amounts of money on so-called Smart Cities under a programme that will impact only a small fraction of the total area of the selected city. We will spend ₹100,000 crore of borrowed money on a bullet train while large parts of the railway infrastructure, like suburban trains and footbridges that are used by the poor, are crumbling or are outdated.

Chasing the dubious goal of a cashless economy we will demonetise 86 per cent of the currency, but callously brush aside the misery and ruin heaped upon millions of people. We will provide vast sums of money to Start-up India and Stand-up India, but turn a blind eye to thousands of small businesses that have perished, taking down with them many thousand jobs.

We will implement the insolvency law with an iron hand but will consign to the dustbin the NFSA. We will spend crores of rupees to promote yoga as the way to a healthier life but we will deny the meagre pension of ₹1,000 per month to old or destitute persons and let them die. (In Tamil Nadu alone there are 2,706,758 applications for pension that have been bundled up because the state government pleads it has no money.)

Where is the place for the poor in the bid to win the approval of Moody's, PEW Research and the World Bank? A rank of 100 in the Ease of Doing Business list is a matter of satisfaction. A rank of 100 in the Hunger list is a matter of shame. The people should never let any government forget that nearly 22 per cent of India's population is still poor and they also have the right to a life of dignity—a truth that Indira Gandhi had acknowledged and defended in her lifetime.

EPILOGUE

2017 was the year in which the Indian economy tanked. Week after week, as I wrote these columns, it was evident that the central government was trapped in a cage of denial, delusion and despair. If the 'start line' of the year was demonetisation, the 'finish line' was the flawed GST (under implementation). The economy bore the brunt of the twin man-made disasters and paid a heavy price. I tracked the course of the economy through the year and was horrified to see how on every key metric the growth rate was on a decline. You—the reader—would have found that walking again through the events of the year is not a pleasant task.

No report card could have been more telling than the result of the election in Gujarat, the home state of Mr Narendra Modi, the prime minister, and Mr Amit Shah, the president of the BJP. Both were the sons of the soil of Gujarat and the state taught them an unforgettable lesson: 'we will let you pass this time, but you are under watch'.

As citizens, as writers, as readers, we have to maintain our vigil. More so in 2018, after the bitter, but totally avoidable, experience of 2017.

ABBREVIATIONS

ABVP	Akhil Bharatiya Vidyarthi Parishad
AFSPA	Armed Forces (Special Powers) Act
AG	Attorney General
AIADMK	All India Anna Dravida Munnetra Kazhagam
ATC	Air Traffic Control
BCTT	Banking Cash Transaction Tax
BE	budget estimates
BJP	Bharatiya Janata Party
CAD	current account deficit
CBI	Central Bureau of Investigation
CEA	Chief Economic Adviser
CPI	Consumer Price Index
CMIE	Centre for Monitoring Indian Economy
CSO	Central Statistics Office
DBT	Direct Benefit Transfer
DGQA	Directorate General of Quality Assurance
DMK	Dravida Munnetra Kazhagam
DPR	Detailed Project Report
DRI	Directorate of Revenue Intelligence
DTC	Direct Taxes Code
EC	Election Commission
ED	Enforcement Directorate
FCRA	Foreign Contribution (Regulation) Act
FICCI	Federation of Indian Chambers of Commerce and Industry

FICN	fake Indian currency note
FPI	Foreign Portfolio Investment
GDP	Gross Domestic Product
GFCF	Gross Fixed Capital Formation
GFP	Goa Forward Party
GSDP	Gross State Domestic Product
GSTN	Goods and Services Tax Network
GVA	Gross Value Added
HDI	Human Development Index
IAP	Integrated Action Plan
IBC	Insolvency and Bankruptcy Code
IFPRI	International Food Policy Research Institute
IIP	Index of Industrial Production
IISc	Indian Institute of Science
J&K	Jammu & Kashmir
JNNURM	Jawaharlal Nehru National Urban Renewal Mission
JNU	Jawaharlal Nehru University
LGBT	Lesbian, gay, bisexual and transgender
LoC	Line of Control
MCI	Medical Council of India
MGNREGS	Mahatma Gandhi National Rural Employment Guarantee Scheme
MGNREGA	Mahatma Gandhi National Rural Employment Guarantee Act
MPC	Monetary Policy Committee
MSMEs	Micro, Small & Medium Enterprises
MSP	minimum support price
MUDRA	Micro units Development and Refinance Agency Ltd.
NATGRID	National Intelligence Grid
NDA	National Democratic Alliance
NFSA	National Food Security Act, 2013
NFHS	National Family Health Survey
NIA	National Investigation Agency
NITI Aayog	National Institution for Transforming India
NPA	non-performing assets

NSA	National Security Advisor
NSAP	National Social Assistance Programme
PDP	Peoples Democratic Party
PMG	Project Monitoring Group
PMGSY	Pradhan Mantri Gram Sadak Yojna
PMLA	Prevention of Money Laundering Act, 2002
PMO	Prime Minister's Office
PSEs	public sector enterprises
RBI	Reserve Bank of India
RE	revised estimates
RNR	revenue neutral rate
RSS	Rashtriya Swayamsevak Sangh
SBI	State Bank of India
SBNs	specified bank notes
SEZs	Special Economic Zones
SFIO	Serious Fraud Investigation Office
UBI	Universal Basic Income
UGC	University Grants Commission
UIDAI	Unique Identification Authority of India
UPA	United Progressive Alliance
VAT	Value Added Tax
VTS	Vehicle Tracking System
WPI	Wholesale Price Index